# NEW TEAMMATE

Matt Winter

Title: *New Teammate*
Copyright © 2023 - Matt Winter

First English edition, June 2023
ISBN: 9798398426267

Instagram: @mattwinter_author

Thank you for purchasing this novel.

# New
# TEAMMATE

Gay erotic novel #

# MATT WINTER

# TABLE OF CONTENTS

# CHAPTER 1

The new one.

How come nobody has told him that bench is off-limits?

"Have you been introduced to Ben yet?" Mark asks, approaching me so drenched in sweat that if you squeeze his T-shirt, a couple of gallons can come out.

"I don't have time today," I reply irritably, heading over to do some dips, leaving him hanging.

I'm already fed up with the new one, and I haven't even met him yet. I disappear from the gym for a month, and my buddies add this guy to the group without even consulting me. They say he's fast, strong, and cool. What athletic skill is "cool"? I think the guys are so bored with their damn lives that any smooth talker can dazzle them with a few easy jokes and a round of beers.

I hop onto the parallel bars and start working my triceps, never taking my eyes off him from the other side of the room. What kind of name is Ben? Benjamin? Bently? Or just Ben?

He's doing bench presses, and carrying a significant amount of weight, but someone should have told him that bench is mine, that no one touches it during this time slot. There are rights that are earned through perseverance, and they're sacred.

He finishes a set and stands up to take a drink of water. He's a tall guy, almost as tall as me, and I have to admit he's in good shape. You have to be to lift that much weight. There's no more than ten percent body fat under that T-shirt. I can't get below twelve percent myself. He must work hard, that's for sure.

I notice that at that moment, he notices me. We're both alone on the mats, even though there are several tens of meters between us. The rest of the people are pounding away on the machines in the other part of the room. At this time of night, in this gym, there are very few of us training.

He raises his hand and greets me through the mirror.

And on top of it all, he's "friendly." Hasn't anyone told him that you don't greet strangers at the gym? I ignore him, fixate on a spot on the mat, and concentrate on my routine.

I don't like that guy.

And I'm very transparent.

# CHAPTER 2

After a hard training session, there's nothing like a good shower.

I admit that I'm a creature of habit: always the same bench, always the same shower stall.

With a towel around my waist and my toiletry bag in hand, I try to enter, but then I realize it's occupied.

Yes.

Indeed.

The new one.

I'm seething with anger. I manage to restrain myself from dragging him out, though that's what he deserves. The other two stalls are occupied, so I have no choice but to enter the only remaining one, which is right in front of the one that was stolen from me by that guy named Ben.

I take a deep breath to try to control myself, although I'm already angry. The cold water gradually calms me down until that unwelcome guy fades from my mind, replaced by the relaxing drowsiness after a long day. Competing in triathlons requires effort, discipline, and endurance, and that must be trained every day, no matter how tired you are.

I begin to soap myself up and turn around so that the stream of water can relieve my trapezius and back. It's a unique sensation, how the icy liquid soothes the muscles, makes the blood circulate faster under the skin and repairs fatigue.

The showers in our gym don't have doors, so I have that Ben guy right in front of me, just a few feet away, with his back turned, his head covered in foam, and just as naked as I am. I think Mark told me he works a few hours restocking shelves at the corner SuperMark and studies I don't know what. At that point, I wasn't paying attention anymore. I start to stare at him because he's the only entertainment I have while my muscles relax. He's massaging his neck, possibly because he hurt himself with so much weight. A guy with that kind of experience should know his limits and not exceed them, because... Yes, I admit he's in good shape.

He has a broad and muscular back, powerful and formed shoulders that stand out under that pale skin. His arms, raised while he massages his neck, contract with big and defined triceps, and matching biceps.

I soap up my chest. To achieve that level of musculature, he must exercise daily, like me, and has been doing so for a long time. He must come from another gym, or perhaps from another city. What did Mark tell me? He was a foreigner, I think, from some unpronounceable place far to the north.

I scan the central line between his shoulder blades that descends down his very pronounced back, framed by dorsal muscles as powerful as the rest, until it reaches his buttocks. I admit they're well-worked. They're big, round, and defined, perfect for running and stabilizing during effort. I soap up my groin while he rinses off, and the white foam seeps through the cleft that separates both buttocks and trickles down the inside of his thighs. He does it slowly, in an almost hypnotic way, stopping occasionally among the slight blond fuzz on his legs.

At that moment, the shampoo bottle slips from his hands and falls to the floor. He bends down to pick it up, and I see beyond, to the shadow of hair that protects the opening. I feel uncomfortable and stop looking. At the gym, we're used to seeing each other naked every day, but that's too intimate. For some reason, my eyes return to that exact and shaded point. He seems to be taking too long to retrieve the bottle, although it's possible he has foam covering his eyes. The same foam that glides down his back and disappears inside, caressing his skin and rushing from the roundness of his testicles, fully exposed, one heavier than the other.

"He's got a pair of good balls," comes to my mind, and I smile at such an absurd thought.

At that moment, at the same time that he turns around, and stares into my eyes.

"Are you guys coming tonight?" It takes me a moment to understand the question. It's Mark, from the adjacent stall.

"Of course," I reply. "Sue made that pie you like."

I finish rinsing off with my back turned, paying no attention to the new guy. He's already pissed me off enough today for him to occupy another second of my thoughts. Only when I step out of the shower, with the towel around my waist, do I have to look at him.

He's still there, water running over his body, unhurried, and I have the feeling that during all that time, he hasn't taken his eyes off me.

# CHAPTER 3

"Damn shitty pass!" Mark shouts and throws his cap against the television.

Dinners at his house are as fun as they are dangerous: too many beers and enough pizza to burst.

We are all seven of us, and we've all come with a girl which, in Rubens' case, it's the one assigned to him this week, and for the rest, it's their wives. We make a good team despite being very different. From Charles, who is a bank director, to Edward, who digs trenches at the railroad construction site. The age range is also diverse. Mark has already passed fifty, Sam hasn't even turned twenty, and I'll be thirty-two next month.

The girls, as always when we gather, have taken over the kitchen, and their laughter can be heard along with the metallic sound of cooking utensils.

The doorbell rings, and Mark gets up.

"It must be Ben. He said they would arrive late."

I furrow my brow but say nothing. I had hoped they hadn't invited the new guy. Someone turns down the volume of the TV as they open the door. I remain seated on one of the two sofas, with my arms stretched out on the backrest and, I suppose, a grim face.

I hear voices at the entrance, one of them a woman's, and some knowing laughter until they appear at the living room door.

The girl is very pretty, brunette, with a pleasant smile and a good figure. The new one has his arm around her shoulder, as if to make it clear that she's his. My eyes wander to his hands, and I realize I'm looking for a ring. There's no sign of one. For some reason, that fact reassures me, even though I'm unable to understand why.

"This is Sharon," he says, introducing her to everyone. "Watch out for the popcorn. She finishes it all."

She laughs and scolds him playfully while the guys welcome her. When she looks at me, I give her a smile that I suspect appeared more like a grimace of displeasure, then I turn my gaze back to the TV screen.

"Come with me, Sharon." Mark, always so polite. "I'll introduce you to the girls. There's plenty of popcorn there."

More laughter, some jokes, and they both disappear toward the kitchen.

Things start to calm down in the living room. Edward is asking the new guy about his training while someone turns up the TV volume again.

I discreetly glance at him. He looks good, I have to admit. Jeans, sneakers, and a well-ironed white shirt. He seems nervous, fidgeting with his hands in his pockets. I've seen him with sweaty and wet hair. Now I notice that it's blond, somewhat dark, and a bit grown out. For some reason, my eyes are drawn to his lips. They have an intense, healthy color, and the lower lip is particularly full. I feel uncomfortable without knowing why. Perhaps because I seem like a spy when all I came here for is to have a few beers.

I return my attention to the TV. Peterson is about to bat, and all my buddies are now focused on the screen.

"Can I sit here?"

I look up. There's the new one, looking at me as he points to the empty space beside me.

"Sure. It's yours," I indicate.

He sits down, almost throwing himself between Charles and me, but he immediately turns toward me.

"You're Jacob."

"The same."

"Ben," he extends his hand.

"I know."

I shake it. He grips tightly while looking into my eyes. I feel something strange, perhaps because he takes longer than necessary to let go, but he immediately smiles again.

"We saw each other yesterday. At the gym."

His image flashes in my mind, his body leaning forward, foam running over his skin, and the shadow of hair between his buttocks. I clear my throat to push away those incomprehensible thoughts.

"Yes." —"Be nice", I tell myself—. "I admit I wasn't very talkative. I'm not much of a talker when I'm tired."

He plays it down with a hand gesture and leans back in the armchair because Peterson failed to hit, and there seems to be a scuffle on the field. The guys comment, but I just take a sip of my beer.

Ben's hair brushes against my bicep, and he doesn't make an effort to move away, although he must be aware of it. It must be a Northern custom, where people are more relaxed than here, because he doesn't bother to maintain a distance between us. His body is practically pressed against mine, to the point where I feel every breath against my skin.

"I heard you've been away," he says, without taking his eyes off the screen, "but they showed me photos so I would know who I'm dealing with."

"Don't trust these guys too much."

He looks at me and smiles. Again, I feel that the gaze lingers for too long.

"Don't worry," he winks at me. "I know what I'm getting into."

He leans back again and settles himself. I get the impression that he has moved even closer to me, to the point where I feel the warmth of his body against mine and the accelerated beating of his heart.

He is talking to Charles about the play, but my mind can't get away from the strange sensation of abnormal contact with Ben's body. I try to concentrate on the game, but it's impossible. There's a pleasant, exciting scent reaching me, and I don't know if it's his shampoo, the fabric softener on his shirt, or some masculine perfume.

I start to get worked up. I don't understand what's happening, why my senses are reacting this way. My brain starts searching for explanations, attributing it all to Ben's relaxed customs, his carefree way of behaving, which clash with the worldview of a Southern bumpkin like me. This idea helps me relax, and the appearance of the girls in the living room bringing food supplies fills the air with funny and saucy comments.

Sue, whom I've been dating for a couple of months, comes straight to us. We met when I saved her from getting her hands dirty because her car broke down in the middle of the road. I thought she was a tourist —everyone knows each other in small towns—, but it turned out she was the new kindergarten teacher. I like blondes, but above all, I like her natural way of dealing with everything.

"So, you're Ben," she says, shaking his hand. "I see you've become good friends with Jacob."

Both of us stand up. Charles snorts; it seems he was uncomfortable with him being so close. That confirms my theory, and I feel my hands relaxing.

"Sit here," I tell Sue.

"No. We're going to the garden. Claire is about to show them what she learned in her belly dance class."

Sharon also approaches, and she hangs onto Ben's neck, planting a kiss on his lips.

"If you're going to attend that impromptu class," he whispers in her ear but loud enough for us to hear, "learn something, because tonight I'm going to ask you to dance it for me."

She laughs and breaks free from his arms with calculated sensuality. Sue seems delighted with the new friends. The girls parade out to the garden through the front door.

"Jacob," my girl says before leaving, "remember that we can't stay too late."

"Don't be a killjoy, Sue," Mark scolds her from his wing chair. "Let him get to know Ben. He's the only one who hasn't fallen under his spell."

Everyone laughs. The new guy does too.

"And you, Ben," Sue knows how to play along, "be careful with this athlete. He bites sometimes."

"I'll keep that in mind," he looks into my eyes for a moment before turning back to Sue immediately, "don't worry."

She leaves, and Ben throws himself back into the armchair, making sure to leave a free space.

No, I'm not sitting next to him again. I can accept foreign customs, but I'm too much of a country guy to share them.

"I'm going for more beers," I pronounce aloud. "Who wants one?"

Hands go up.

And I head towards the kitchen because I need a few seconds alone.

# CHAPTER 4

"I don't think you can handle everything."

When I turn around, there's Ben. He has followed me into the kitchen and stands by the central island, his hands in the back pockets of his pants. There's a certain discomfort in him, evident in his inability to stand still.

"I was planning to make a couple of trips," I reply.

"Give me that."

He takes some bottles from my hands and sets them on the counter, effortlessly opening two using the handle of a fork. He hands one to me and keeps the other for himself.

"Why do you think we don't get along?" he raises his bottle for a toast.

I clink my bottle against his, but I know my forehead is furrowed.

"What makes you think that?"

He smiles slightly and brushes his blond hair away from his forehead, shrugging his shoulders.

"I have the impression that you don't like me very much."

I feel uncomfortable, as if I've done something wrong.

"I already told you. When I'm tired, I use few words."

He takes a long, slow sip, savoring the bitter liquid. I find myself staring at his throat. The Adam's apple moves up and down beneath his pale skin, which possesses a delicate yet rugged quality.

"Mark has told me about you," he declares when he finishes.

"Mark talks too much," I protest.

"He says you work at Rockblack's carpentry."

"I grew up there."

Ben leans on the counter and licks the foam from the edge of his lips with his tongue. He's staring at me intently while he does it, and I'm not entirely sure if he's looking into my eyes, at my mouth, or going from one to the other, in a triangle that creates a strange sensation for me. Almost disturbing.

"Sharon wants a custom-made shelf for the laundry room," he sets the beer aside. "She says putting things on top of the washing machine brings bad luck."

I clear my throat, because my mind is racing, wondering what the hell is wrong with me and why I feel restless in the presence of the new guy.

"I can come by to take measurements and give you an estimate," I say, more to get through the conversation than with any intention of actually doing it. "I wouldn't charge you for the labor."

"That would be great," he crosses his arms, and his biceps bulge beneath his shirt. "We're tight on money."

We both stand there, motionless, looking into each other's eyes as if searching for an answer. I think about how absurd it would be if someone walked in and caught us like this, like two statues left haphazardly in the kitchen.

"Mark also told me you put in a few hours at Supermark," I try to change the subject.

"As many as I can. Sharon and I have been together for a year, but we have plans. For now, we're managing with my savings until she finishes college. Then..., we'll see."

A smile forms on my face, and I see him mirroring it when he notices.

"I don't remember our town having a college."

"I'm doing it remotely," he blushes, I think. "And there are affordable houses in this area, so I only travel for exams."

"What are you studying?"

"Law."

"A shyster" my eyebrows raise on their own.

"And I owe you one," he winks at me, "for the shelf, so when I get my license, count on a free defense."

He puts a hand on my shoulder and leaves it there, while his eyes remain fixed on mine. I feel the warmth of his fingers through my shirt and a strange tingling sensation in the back of my neck. He swallows hard. He's nervous. I know it. But... why?

"The guys must be thirsty," I reply abruptly.

I grab four beers and head back to the living room without looking back. The guys are where I left them, still engaged in the same debate about whether Peterson should retire or hold on for another season.

"Beers for everyone."

Applause and cheers as they take the bottles from my hands.

"About time. I was going to drink the vase."

Ben appears with the bottles rest of the beers and hands me the one he had opened for me.

"This one, and I'm out of here, or Sue will drag me by the balls. She invited me to dinner at her house tonight."

"Party pooper," Mark protests from his wing chair, where it's difficult to move him on game days.

Ben approaches a little closer, just enough.

"Stay."

I have the feeling that he's begging me.

"I have training tomorrow, and I need to hit it hard," I say loudly, for everyone to hear, to break any trace of intimacy.

"Tomorrow?" he looks surprised. "It's Sunday."

"Old man Bill lets him use the keys," clarifies Mark, who is a loudmouth.

I feel uneasy again. I don't know. Nothing is happening, but this guy evokes sensations in me that I can't quite comprehend.

"I have to make up for a month where all I did was run," I find myself making excuses.

Ben looks at me and then at the others.

"Can I train with you?" he says to me and the group.

"What a great idea!" Charles agrees.

"Tomorrow?" I ask, unsure of what to say.

"I need to catch up with you guys," he explains. "Besides, this way we'll get to know each other a bit more. You're the only one I haven't trained with."

Everyone thinks it's a cracking idea, so I have no choice but to accept.

"Okay. Sure."

"Is ten o'clock a good time?"

I head towards the door. I want to be at home, with my girl naked in bed.

"Come whenever you want. I'll be there a little earlier."

# CHAPTER 5

I'm training when I hear Ben come in. I left the latch of the gate open so that he doesn't have to call and interrupt me in the middle of my workout.

Our old gym is nothing like those on television, with machines that measure visceral fat and retained fluids. It's old-fashioned, a large and open building, a few blocks outside the town, where Old Bill has placed machines and weights, and for the last couple of years, a twenty-five-meter indoor pool that is the pride of the county.

"You're sweating," he says approaching me and throwing his backpack on the floor. "What time did you arrive?"

"A while ago."

I'm actually already on my last sets. I came earlier than necessary, not sure why, as Sue and I don't have any plans today, and I could stay here until lunchtime.

Ben is wearing very short shorts and a tight tank top. Despite all the machines being free, he sits on the bench next to mine. He also has sweat stains on his chest and back, so I assume he came running to warm up.

Without saying anything, he starts working on his joints to get them ready before adding weight. I continue with my routine, a full-body workout today, trying to ignore him. I don't feel like talking, nor do I want to get too close. There's something about him that throws me off balance.

"I hate lunges," he says, referring to the exercise I'm doing.

I look at him. He started with squats, and I marvel at his refined technique that allows him to lower himself to the ground with a completely straight back.

"There's nothing more effective for hip flexibility," I reply.

"Do you have problems with that?"

I look at him again. There's a grimace of humor on his mouth.

"No, I don't," I answer, very seriously. "But it was on the schedule for today."

Silence falls between us again. I suspect he is gauging how far he can go with his familiarity, and I am not about to make it easy for him. We barely make any noise as we lift weights. I curse myself for not putting on some music; that would have made this moment less tense.

Ben has started doing pull-ups. I know he's looking at me when he thinks I'm not looking, perhaps because I do the same when he's turned around. Between repetitions, he paces up and down, practices some boxing moves, and does push-ups. When he finishes his sets, he returns to the bench next to me.

"It was a shame you left yesterday."

"Sue was tired," and it's true, "and I wanted to get up early."

"We had a good time."

"I'm glad."

I'm doing bench press, loaded up with discs, and the last thing I want to do is talk. Today, I intend to hit a new personal record, and I have to stay focused. I look at him from the corner of my eye and see him approaching me.

"Can I help you?" he asks.

"It's not necessary."

"Let me," he insists, "you'll be more secure."

I decide it's better not to protest, and a helping hand wouldn't hurt. I lie down fully on the bench, and Ben places himself at the head to hold the bar when I push.

I prepare, plant my feet, arch my back, and grip the bar tightly. He moves a little closer and also holds it with both hands, but he puts them so close to mine that they touch. I feel like an electric shock, so deep that I raise my head. What's just twenty centimeters away from my face is his crotch. His shorts have shifted, revealing the curve of his buttocks. I look at the sweaty lining where the line that separates both cheeks is perfectly defined, and I feel my face burning. Once again, I feel confused. I grip tightly and lift the bar. He makes the same effort and has to move forward just enough to widen that view, only centimeters away from my eyes.

My head spins, trying to understand what's happening to me. I lower the bar with a clang and sit up.

"That was great," he says enthusiastically.

I jump to my feet and grab my towel.

"I'm going to the shower," I announce without further ado. "I left the keys next to the door. When you're done, just turn off the lights and lock up."

He looks at me with a furrowed brow. He probably doesn't understand anything. I don't understand it either, why I feel so confused, uncomfortable. I've seen my buddies' sweaty crotch countless times, and I've never stared at it. Why did I now investigate, almost desiring it to stay above me for a few more moments?

I push those dark thoughts out of my head and leave him alone.

I need a cold shower.

# CHAPTER 6

The cold water calms me, although my mind remains restless. It searches for an explanation for what just happened. I looked at a guy's ass and got turned on. That's the reality. I can't find the reason why it happened. I've never been attracted to men or noticed them before. Why now, with the new guy...?

"I don't want to push myself further today," Ben's voice sounds. "My trapezius muscles are sore, and I don't want to get injured."

I open my eyes, and there he is, on the other side, occupying the adjacent shower stall, just like last time. Apparently, he has decided to finish his workout. He has a complete lack of modesty about his nudity, and I dare say he enjoys exposing his perfect body to me.

I don't answer anything. I simply turn my back, feeling a certain modesty, as if now, after half a lifetime in locker rooms, I'm ashamed of someone seeing my dick.

My senses are heightened, trying to guess his movements by the sound of water on his skin. I feel the hair on my back stand on end, as if there's an electric current, and I resist a voice telling me to turn around, to look him in the eyes without averting my gaze, to finally discover what the hell is going on between that guy and me.

Suddenly, his voice sounds just inches from my ear.

"I'm out of shampoo. I dropped the damn bottle yesterday. Do you mind if I use yours?"

I spin around. He's there, inside my shower stall, looking at me while brushing his wet bangs away from his forehead.

"S-sure," I stammer like an idiot.

He reaches out to grab the bottle from the shelf and brushes against my side, as if it were unavoidable. He also gets too close. The electric sensation coursing through my body intensifies. So much so that his naked body is just centimeters away from mine. I'm paralyzed, like when you know something is about to happen and you're not sure how you're going to react. He takes too long, or time has stood still.

At that moment, he lowers his head.

"Oh," he says, and bites his juicy lower lip.

I also look down, and I see that my dick has reacted just like my skin, growing and thickening a few centimeters.

I say nothing. I don't even dare to move, although I notice that my breathing has accelerated.

Slowly, very slowly, Ben gets down on his knees.

On his knees.

And I still don't move, don't dare to say anything, even though I know what he's going to do. And I hate it. And I desire it. And my dick grows a little more just imagining it. Contrary to everything believable, that possibility still excites me even more. It also confuses me like I've never been before.

I follow his gestures, hypnotized by what is happening. I see how he's been staring at my dick, just inches away from his face, in all its fullness, with hunger in his eyes. I've always been well-endowed, but today it seems larger, with the veins that characterize me even more pronounced under pressure.

Slowly, Ben approaches and, with a tenderness that elicits a painful desire in my balls, he kisses it. It's just a brush. A gesture with his lips, and then with the tip of his tongue. But he does it in a way that sends a shiver of pleasure through me.

He seems satisfied with the result and takes it into his mouth. I hold my breath as he starts to suck. He knows what he's doing and how to do it. It's his lips and tongue, wetting, absorbing, sucking, while his other hand massages my balls.

Pleasure washes over me in waves. I've never been sucked off this well. The right pressure, precise licks that drive me crazy. I tighten my glutes and thrust my hips forward as I watch him devour it, enjoying himself, while his free hand jerks himself off. That only excites me more, to the point where I know I'm about to cum any moment.

He seems to realize it because he quickens the movements of his tongue, sucking deeper, to the point where I'm overwhelmed with pleasure.

When the orgasm hits, I know it's the deepest one of my life. Pleasure pierces and tears through me, from a part of myself I didn't know existed.

Involuntarily, I grip the new one's head tightly, driving my dick deeper, until it's lodged in his throat while he chokes on the stream of spunk. He tries to pull away, gasping for air, because my dick is filling his entire mouth, but I don't let him. I cum right there, with the full length of my dick buried in him, until the last spasm shakes me.

Only then do I let go, and he falls to the side, supported by one hand on the gray stone floor, coughing and spitting semen from his throat and nose.

I try to gather myself, to make sense of what just happened, but my legs weaken.

I stumble out of the shower, while he also tries to recover on the gray stone floor.

My head is a whirlwind where guilt, incomprehension, and memories of desire mix into an inexplicable cocktail.

I hurriedly get dressed, awkwardly, and even as I put on my shirt, I leave the gym, because I find myself unable to look at the new one in the face again.

# CHAPTER 7

I arrive at Sue's house so disturbed that she notices something is wrong.

"Did you argue with Ben?" she assumes.

"No."

"Then what's the matter with you?"

I don't answer and go out to the patio to chop wood. With each swing of the axe, it feels like I'm the one splitting in half. How could I have allowed it? How did I let myself? I'm not a fag, and I don't like men. I excuse myself by thinking that I didn't do anything, that it was him, that... but my resistance was nonexistent.

In addition to the guilt, the memory of desire and pleasure pierces through me. It was an epic orgasm. I don't recall another one of that intensity, not even that night with the two dancers that left my balls so empty that I couldn't jerk off for a week.

With each strike, I feel a little calmer, although what happened doesn't leave my mind.

Sue seems to have forgotten the bad mood I arrived with at her house, because lunch and the after-dinner are like every Sunday. The difference lies in the fact that when the word "END" appears in the movie we've been watching, cuddled on the couch, I realize that I have no fucking idea what the hell we watched, because my mind was occupied with all this shit.

My parents and my nephews ease our afternoon. Mom notices that something is wrong with me, but I attribute it to work. When they leave, it's very late, and we go to bed.

Sue presses her body against mine, looking to get laid. I don't feel like it because the memory of this morning's orgasm still tortures me, but I realize that it's a good way to measure myself, to discover what the hell happened to me.

I fuck her in such a wild way, thrusting deep inside her, stopping when I'm about to cum to make it last longer. By the time we finally finish, she has come a couple of times and looks at me with bright eyes.

"I haven't had this much fun in a long time," she tells me.

I kiss her lips and turn around to sleep.

But I sleep little and poorly. The new one appears in my dream, his juicy lips, the way I saw them wrapped around my dick, the way he caressed my balls. And when I wake up in the morning, I see that my underwear is stuck to me, with a stain of dried semen.

When I arrive at work, I go straight to my boss's office.

"Is there any work out of town?" I ask him from the doorway, leaning against the frame with my fingers on the belt loops.

"Are you serious?" he looks at me surprised. "You messed me up last month when I sent you to work in Illinois for four weeks to set up those houses."

I shrug.

"I could use some extra money, and you paid for the travel and expenses."

"If you need an advance..."

"I need to be away for a few days."

My boss looks into my eyes, his forehead wrinkled. He's a good guy, tough, but he doesn't meddle in anything.

"One week, in the South. We need to supervise a lumber shipping."

"That works for me. Can I leave tomorrow?"

"Is everything okay, Jacob?"

"Everything's perfect."

He analyzes me again, wondering if he should be concerned.

"Tomorrow is a good day."

I turn around without saying anything else. Tonight, I'll have to explain it to Sue, but she'll understand in the end.

At least this week without seeing the new one will allow me to sort things out.

# CHAPTER 8

"Can I talk to you?"

Ben is restocking products on a shelf in the supermarket, and when he hears my voice, he turns so quickly that the coffee packages end up on the floor. Neither he nor I make any effort to pick them up. At this time of day, there are few people in the supermarket, so we have some privacy in the candy and snacks aisle.

"I heard you were working away again," he says.

"For a week. I just got back."

He questions me with his eyes, but my expression is quite impenetrable. I feel my heart beating strongly, and my palms are sweaty, but I've made up my mind to make things clear, and it has to happen today.

"In the back alley," he nods his head. "Give me five minutes to let the manager know."

I nod and head over there. The only Chinese restaurant in town and the most well-known pizzeria are in the same alley, so it smells of spicy food, filling the big containers two by two.

I stand there with my hands in my pockets and my hoodie zipped up to my neck. I just saw him bending over, unaware that I was behind him, and I felt that strange rush again, not knowing if it's desire or madness.

Ben appears shortly after. He looks worried. He's wearing white pants and the tight blue polo shirt that's part of the uniform. He must have worked out before lunch, because his biceps are still pumped.

"Is everything okay?" he says, not getting too close.

I decide not to beat around the bush. I know very well what I came here to say.

"The other day, in the showers..."

"I wanted to apologize," he cuts me off.

In a way, I appreciate that he also understood that it was a mistake.

"It wasn't right," I try to explain, "I'm not..."

"Me neither."

That surprises me. The word "fag" is stuck in my mouth. But it was him, not me, who started it. But it was him, not me, who started it, it was him who followed me to the shower, who got into my shower, who...

"You ate my dick," I say with acrimony.

"So what?"

I'm taken aback. Apparently, eating a guy's dick is as common as brushing your teeth. The good vibe I brought with me starts to fade.

"I don't care what anyone is," I try to calm myself, "I've never meddled in anyone's life, and I won't do it now, but that's not my thing."

"Fine."

His responses confuse me. He's standing there, hands in his pockets, with rosy cheeks. Handsome as hell, and he agrees with me while simultaneously taking it away because his way of looking at me isn't innocent. I saw him glance at my package a couple of times, and his eyes move from mine to my lips. All of this confuses me, it spins me around.

"If you think so," I try to put an end to it, "we won't talk about this again."

He nods.

"We'll pretend it never happened if that's what you want," he says very seriously.

Now I'm the one nodding my head. It's done. I can go back home, give Sue a couple of kisses, and get on with my life. This was just a story to tell while drunk at a bar: a guy ate my dick at the gym at the gym. We'll laugh, toast, and someone else will tell another joke of the same kind.

"That was it," I conclude. "I've done what I came to do. I saw you as I passed by and thought it was important to clarify. I'm leaving. I still haven't seen Sue."

He nodded and raised his hand in a farewell gesture but didn't say anything.

I stood there for a few seconds, silent, unable to take my eyes off his. I swallowed hard and turned around, heading towards the road at the end of the alley. My head ached, and it felt like every muscle in my body was tense.

All of this is strange, very strange. So strange that I can't find an explanation. If this had happened with someone else, not only would I have put a stop to it in time, but I probably would have punched them in the face. But with the new one...

I came to a sudden halt. What am I doing? And I turned back.

Ben was still there, unmoving, as if he had been watching me as I walked away. Leaning against the railing of the staircase that led to the supermarket, hands in his pockets, he observed me approaching with curiosity.

"Why did you do it?" I rebuked him when I reached his side again.

He let it out without hesitation.

"Because I like you."

I was shocked, furrowed my brow, and clenched my fists.

"What the hell is that?"

He didn't back down. He shrugged but looked at me with the same clarity as a moment ago.

"I go with the flow and enjoy it," he pointed to me with his chin. "Didn't you enjoy it?"

I've been hard all week just thinking about the blowjob this bastard gave me, but I can't let him take me to his level.

"We're not talking about that," I clarified.

He smiled, and a shiver ran down my spine. He ran his hand over his mouth and looked at me intently, with his head slightly lowered, making him incredibly seductive.

"The orgasm was amazing. My throat still hurts."

My mouth went dry. I couldn't erase from my mind the image of my dick embedded there while the spunk gushed out, and the pleasure stabbed my kidneys.

"I'm not into these things," I defended myself, but my voice cracked.

He straightened up, and in doing so, he was closer to me. Very close to me. So close that I just had to lean my head to kiss him.

"And how do you know?" he challenged me.

"Because I can guarantee that you enjoyed it as much as I did. And I assure you, with that dick you have, I enjoyed it a lot."

Sweaty hands and a racing heart. That's how I get when I'm with this guy.

"I know, and that's that," I replied.

He took a step towards me. Only a few inches of air between him and me. If someone appeared, they would notice. That there's something strange between the new guy and me. That scares me because I'm not like this.

"I know you want to get rid of all that shit in your head," he said, "and I assure you one thing. There's only one way."

"What way?"

He bit his lower lip. It has a hypnotic effect on me because I can't take my eyes off it. His eyes hesitated, but in the end, he dared.

"Let's do it again."

I pushed him, but he was strong, and he only moved a couple of steps back.

"Fuck off."

He pointed at me.

"I know what's going through your head because I've been there. You can resist as much as you want, even for the rest of your life, but it won't go away."

I raise my fist and threaten him.

"I'm going to..."

"Hit me if you want," he interrupts fearlessly. "Ignore it or try it again. Maybe this time it will disgust you, make you sick, make you hate it, or it won't get you hard. If that happens, it'll all be over. It was just a heat of the moment and a mouth, in the end, is a mouth."

"I don't want you to come near me again," I warn him slowly, leaving no doubt that I'm dangerous.

He steps back. His gaze is expressionless. Mine, furious.

"I have to get back to work," he tells me. "Nothing happened between you and me, so you shouldn't worry. But I'll tell you one thing... I won't be the one to take the next step."

And he goes back inside without looking back, leaving me with my fist in the air.

# CHAPTER 9

For two days, I don't show up at the gym and dedicate myself to running in the countryside. I don't want to see him, I don't want to run into him, I don't want to know anything about him.

On the third day, Mark calls me.

"Where the hell have you been?"

"I'm doing some repairs at home."

I make an excuse, although I told Sue that I'm not going to the gym because Old Bill is fixing the showers.

"Jacob, we're a team," he complains. "If we're not all there, it won't work."

"It's only for a couple of weeks, it'll be fine."

There's a moment of silence on the phone, something unthinkable when talking to Mark, who always has something to say.

"Has something happened between you and Ben?" he suddenly asks.

The hairs on the back of my neck stand up. Has it been that obvious, or did he let the cat out of the bag?

"Why do you say that?" I probe.

"I don't know. He used to ask a lot about you. Now it seems like you don't exist."

"What kind of things did he ask?"

I regret showing interest. If any of the guys suspect something, I must not give them any cause for it.

"The usual stuff," he replies. "Who you were, what you did for a living, if you were married," I hear him grumbles. "You have a shitty attitude, and you know it. I'm sure you've been tough on the boy."

I feel relieved. It was just curiosity. Normal curiosity about the missing piece in a close-knit team and whom he didn't yet know. Or is it something else?

"Nothing like that has happened," I reassure him. "We've barely exchanged a few words."

"Well, come tomorrow for training."

"I will."

The next day, I meet up with the guys after work, as usual. It's swimming day, and old Bill lets us have the pool to ourselves after closing to the public.

We haven't seen each other since the dinner at Mark's house, and that was less than two weeks ago. In the locker room, as we change, the guys high-five me and pat my back as if I've been gone for a year. I don't ask about Ben, but he's not there.

I put on my Turbo swimsuit, cap, and goggles, and head to the pool. I admit I'm in good shape. Very good, actually. I've always had a broad back and well-developed muscles. Swimming has given me these arms and chest, and running has sculpted my legs. I've had a beard for as long as I can remember, I buzz my hair short because it's thick and strong and, according to my mother, I inherited the black hair and tanned skin from dad's family, while the blue eyes are solely hers. Mother's things, but they never lie.

When I arrive at the pool, one of the lanes is occupied. It's Ben, who arrived before the rest and glides through the water with long, agile strokes, his impressive physique perfectly executed in each stroke.

That damn tightness between my ribs returns, but I pretend and start warming up before diving into the water, while the guys enter and share their damn jokes, which are always the same.

No can't take my eyes off Ben, although I pretend to have them lost somewhere. He does the crawl on the way there and backstroke on the way back, giving me a complete view of his body from behind and then from the front. I observe how his buttocks move in and out in rhythm with his legs, barely concealed by a very small white swimsuit. The line separating them is perfectly defined, darkening as it goes deeper. On the way back, I realize that his package also shows its shadow, a pubic area that I glimpsed in the shower, covered by a timid layer of blond hair.

I notice that I'm starting to get semi-hard, so I quickly dive into the water before the guys notice. The exercise helps me forget all that, Ben and the tantalizing vision of his body. I push myself hard, swimming lap after lap without resting, feeling my muscles tense and respond until I'm so tired that the last strokes are a struggle.

I get out of the pool and sit on the curb. When I look around, I realize that I'm alone, and only when I manage to fix my gaze on the huge wall clock do I realize that I've been swimming for an hour and a half, and everyone has already left.

I sigh. Better this way. And I head towards the showers.

Mark is in front of the mirror, combing his thick hair.

"Damn, you really pushed yourself, man."

"I needed it."

"Remember that tomorrow is the Black Mountain thing."

I had completely forgotten. The guys have been talking about it for two months.

"Yeah, don't worry," I excuse myself.

Three of the showers are occupied, so I enter the only available one.

I take off my swimsuit, remove my cap and goggles, and step under the stream of cold water.

Only when I turn around do I come face to face with Ben, just like the previous times. But this time something has changed, because he doesn't look at me, he doesn't seem to notice me.

He's standing sideways, with his eyes closed, one hand resting against the wall as he enjoys the hot water and a light cloud of steam envelops him.

I stare at him, mesmerized. He is stunningly beautiful. Every muscle is slightly defined, with just the right size, the appropriate density, and perfect shape. And then there are his buttocks. The profile presents two juicy semispheres to me, slightly pink, splashed with red where the water is very hot.

I desire him.

And I curse myself.

I imagine my face, my mouth, my tongue between those cheeks, and I curse myself again.

I cover myself with my hand and with the foam, because my dick starts to react to everything I'm thinking. I hide it when Charles leaves the adjacent shower and says goodbye before leaving, in case I take too long. When Edward vacates the next shower, we are the only two left, facing each other, wet and naked.

But he doesn't seem to notice my presence, and if he does, he doesn't show it.

With the tip of my index finger lubricated by soap, I stroke my glans in long circles, following the swollen curb, until I stop at the tip and intensify the caress there.

Ben opens his eyes, but he doesn't look at me. I stop and pretend, covering myself with more foam as if I were thoroughly washing between my legs. But once again, he ignores me, leaves the shower, and goes away.

I furrow my brow and feel bad.

I don't know what the hell is happening to me. Maybe I'm going through a horny phase, and I get hard even by a guy with a nice ass. I laugh at my own thought, but instead of enjoying the shower, I turn off the tap and head towards the lockers.

I try to deny it, but I'm doing it to see him again. I know it. And it bothers me. And it confuses me.

When I arrive, Charles finishes putting on his sweatshirt while talking about the Black Mountain thing with Edward, who is tying his boots.

"Has everyone already left?" I ask, when what I really wanted to say is "Where's Ben?"

"It's just the three of us left," Edward replies. "And hurry up, because today I'm the one responsible for the keys."

# CHAPTER 10

To Black Mountain we go to get drunk.

It's a small town in the mountains that keeps its peaks snow-covered all year round and that authentic charm we love so much.

The excuse for coming here every year is different; this time, there's an agricultural fair, and Mark's company is exhibiting their harvesters. But ever since they started doing it, we've taken advantage of that weekend to spend time together as a family, to bond as a group that trains hard every damn day of the year, that competes every three or four months, and that needs a moment where we just want to have fun... and get drunk.

We're going in two cars, although we agreed to meet directly at the hotel, because Charles, the one I'm going with, can't leave until noon, and Mark has to be there before ten.

The journey flies by with jokes, pranks, and lots of country music playing. When we arrive, the other four are already in the hotel bar, drinking beer.

"You're three rounds behind," says Mark, raising his glass.

"Don't worry about that," Charles challenges him. "I'll beat you before the night is over."

Ben is talking to Edward about his diaphragmatic breathing technique, something oriental that the rest of us don't bother to understand, and he doesn't notice me. He seems relaxed and happy, and he's the only one with a full beer.

"It was a random draw," explains Mark, who has a bunch of magnetic keys in his hand. "I ended up with Martin, so I get the worst deal."

"Bullshit," says his roommate with humor. "You snore, so you better not do it tonight." He hands him a card. "Charles and Edward, you two are together."

I look at Ben. I wonder who he'll end up with. When we travel, I always share a room with Rubens. We get along well, and we both have a laid-back vibe. I assume it'll be the same this time, so he'll be paired with Sam. I feel a strange... jealousy? That surprises me so much that the bartender has to hand me a beer for the third time, which I didn't even order, but apparently, it's part of the welcome.

The bellhop has taken our suitcases, so we don't need to go to the room. Mark's thing. He's all about not wasting a second.

"Sam," our host continues, handing out the last magnetic keys, "this time you're with Rubens. So, Jacob and Ben, you'll be sharing a room."

Ben nods, but doesn't look at me and continues the conversation as if nothing happened.

"To an unforgettable weekend," Mark raises his glass once the rooms have been assigned.

We all toast. I notice that my heart beats faster than usual, and even though I try not to, my eyes occasionally wander to Ben as if they need him.

But the new one ignores me. Well, not exactly. He responds when I speak, even directs his words to me, but with an indifference that annoys me when I realize he treats everyone the same way.

More beers, sausages, pork knuckles, and boiled cabbage arrive. Noon turns into the evening, the hotel bar turns into a nearby cocktail lounge, and that becomes a nightclub when the clock strikes twelve, and we suddenly remember that we haven't had dinner.

"Another year missing out on dinner," someone says.

I haven't drunk much. The trick is to bring the glass to your lips without drinking, so that the level of the glass doesn't go down, and you don't have to endure refills. I'm not one to get drunk, and I feel uneasy about having to sleep in the same room as Ben, although with his attitude towards me and the drunken state he's in, I doubt I have anything to fear.

The afternoon and evening have passed in the same manner: the new one only interacts with me when necessary, but I can't recall a single time he looked at me. I'm overwhelmed by conflicting feelings. On one hand, I feel calm because it seems all that sexual stuff is behind us. On the other hand, I feel unsettled because, somewhere deep inside me, there might still be a lingering heat for the strange and risky game we were playing.

When Charles and Rubens started vomiting on the stage where two Russians were playing the accordion, we concluded that we were done for the day.

Black Mountain is small, and we can carry them to the hotel on piggyback. We say our goodbyes at the elevators, although the boys are so drunk that I doubt they even know how to open the door with the keycard.

Ben and I are left alone, because our room is the last one at the end of a long hallway. He staggers in front of me. I keep an eye in case I need to help him, but he reaches the door with some dignity. Opening it is another story, but on the fourth try, the lock makes an electronic sound, and it opens.

As I check the suitcases left at the entrance, I hear Ben's voice.

"Damn, they made a mistake."

When I enter the room, I understand what he means. There's only one double bed instead of two, as it was supposed to be.

"I'll go down to reception to let them know," he says with a slurred voice, but when he tries to move, he falls onto the bed.

I realize he's in no condition to do anything.

"For tonight, let's leave it like this," I resign myself. "I don't think you can stay awake until they prepare another room. We'll fix it first thing in the morning."

He nods. He's lying on his back, and everything indicates he can't sit up. I feel uncomfortable. I look around; if only there were a sofa, I'd leave him there, covered with a blanket. But he's occupying the entire center of the bed, and I don't intend to sleep on the carpet. I decide to be practical.

"Come on," I tell him. "I'm going to help you undress and get into bed."

He smiles, or at least I think he does.

I gather my patience and unbutton his shirt. Ben keeps his eyes closed, and I take the opportunity to look at him. He's stunningly beautiful, and my eyes get stuck on his lips, red and moist from alcohol.

I shake my head to dismiss those shady thoughts.

I manage to sit him up, although he's quite heavy, and I struggle to take off his shirt. Then I focus on his pants. I unbutton his belt, unzip the button, and lower the fly. He's wearing white briefs, and the shape of his dick creates a high relief where the glans perfectly outlined. I run my hand over my mouth and look away. He kicked off his shoes when he lay down, or maybe they went flying, I can't remember. I sit him up a bit and manage to pull his pant legs down just enough to slide them off.

Now he's only wearing his underwear. The incredibly pale skin, the defined muscles, the light, blond hair on his legs, just like the tuft of hair that emerges from his belly button and disappears into the waistband of his briefs. His posture, with his arms and legs spread open, is as if he's offering himself, as if he's saying, "come here," and my neck tingles so much that I swallow and lean against the wall.

Of all the things that could go wrong this weekend, this was the most terrible and improbable: that Ben would end up naked in my bed, and here he is.

I almost feel like laughing. I still have to tuck him into the sheets, but I need to take a shower, wash away this heated sensation enveloping me, and rid myself of him.

I enter the bathroom and leave him there. The heating is on, and it won't get cold. The shower relaxes me and eases the heat in my kidneys, which extends to my balls. I don't have pajamas, because I never wear them, so I put on my boxer briefs and return to the room.

I stop at the threshold, and again a sensation runs down my spine from the exact point where the testicles end and the dick begins.

Ben is still lying on the bed, but he has turned face down, and perhaps due to the alcohol fumes or discomfort, he has removed his underwear and is completely naked.

I stare at that strong back, with well-defined dorsal muscles and powerful scapulas, the line that surrounds the spine, the narrow, tight waist, and I fixate on that round and delicious ass, delicious and round, and on the soft crack that deepens as it's covered by a light and surely soft hair.

And I come to the conclusion that it's going to be a very long night.

# CHAPTER 11

The night passes in a light sleep state full of strange dreams. In some of them, I make love to Ben, but when I wake up, he's still sleeping, covered by the sheet and turned to the other side.

Dawn begins to break when I finally open my eyes and silently thank myself for not getting drunk yesterday. Immediately, his image comes to mind, naked in my bed, and I turn around to check that I'm not dreaming again.

However, there's no one there. Only I am in the bed, covered by the sheet up to my waist. I sit up. Is it possible that I dreamed it all? That I dreamt of undressing him during the night while he remained semi-conscious in bed?

The bathroom door opens, and Ben appears, freshly showered, with a towel wrapped around his waist.

"I needed a shower," he says.

He looks into my eyes for a moment, but quickly looks away. I didn't hear the water running, but it was such a tumultuous night, with so many strange ideas swirling in my head that I suppose I must have fallen into a deep sleep.

"I need one too," I verbalize, my voice sounding guttural.

I'm about to get up when he sits on the bed right next to me.

"Was it you who undressed me?" he asks me, quite serious.

"You had been drinking. I figured you would be more comfortable without clothes."

He nods. He's very close, and his eyes analyze mine.

"And was it necessary to take off my underwear?"

I feel myself blush... Did he think...?

"You took care of that yourself."

He tries to remember, and eventually succeeds. I can't get up, because he's sitting on the sheet that covers my legs, and too close.

"Did we...?" he leaves it hanging.

"Of course not!" I exclaim.

And then he kisses me.

It's a quick gesture. He leans his head forward, and our lips meet only to separate immediately.

He keeps looking at me, very serious, until a sigh of pain escapes him.

"I promised myself I wouldn't make the first move, but yesterday it was so hard having you so close."

I swallow hard. I'm petrified. My mind searches for an exit that it can't find.

"I thought you had forgotten about what happened between us," my lips say, unsure if it was really me who spoke.

"That's impossible," he smiles, sweet and tender. "I can't get you out of my head."

I reach out a hand and hold him by the back of his neck.

He stares at me.
I into his eyes.
He's not sure if I'm about to hit him.
Me either.

But my need is so strong, the desire coursing through my spine like a swarm of wasps, that I pull him towards me and plunge into his mouth.

I sigh against his lips as my tongue explores, caresses, and discovers if that juicy shape matches what I imagined. And he's surprised because it's even more delicious, tastier, and full of sensations.

Ben also sighs when he realizes I'm kissing him. He removes the towel and straddles me.

Our chests rub against each other. My nipples press against his skin, and the dense hair on my pecs brushes and rubs against his light, blond chest hair.

My hips and my hands, which have lowered down there to accommodate him, to move him slightly so that he sits just right on my dick, they all feel it too.

Only a few cotton microns in the form of a sheet separate us. The rest is given over to each other.

We caress each other while our mouths search and find. They suck to beat a retreat and instantly return to the fray.

I flip him over to lay him on the bed and rip the sheet off me.

I look into his eyes for a moment before getting on top of him. They are bright, warm inviting.

He opens his mouth and I accept the challenge.

Carefully, I lay down on his body. I feel our knees rub slightly. That his thighs support the weight of mine. I rip off my boxers and adjust his stance more, feeling my thick, knobby dick caress his slightly smaller, softer one.

That intimate contact turns me on even more and I throw myself back into his mouth. I want to kiss him until I cum, touch him until I cum, lick him until I cum.

Our hands feverishly seek places where they have not yet landed, while we both move our hips, in search of greater contact, greater pleasure.

I have to stop and step away slightly, because my spunk is screaming to come out, but I need it to last longer.

I have a plan, and I am about to fulfill it.

I kiss her chin. I bite his tip on the chin and go down to his neck. He groans and tries to stop me, but I'm stronger and immobilize his hand.

I go down to his clavicle, I run my tongue over it, it's salty and it smells like lemon. He continued down and I faced his nipples. They are surrounded by soft blond hair. He traced her areola with his tongue. He twists between my lips, prisoner of pleasure, but I don't stop. I open my mouth and swallow his nipple. I play with it, I suck it, I nibble it. Between my lips it grows and hard until he arches his back and I'm afraid he's going to cum. So, I stop and descend a little more.

He forced me to kiss him, and soon find myself close to his dick.

I have never had one so few inches from my lips. I pull away to look at her. It is big, although not as big as mine, compact, with a bluish vein that runs through it. I smell it. The soap has erased the masculine imprint, but in the background that macho smell, of leather, of semen, can still be appreciated.

I keep going down, the testicles that aroused me so much expand before me. I stick my nose in and inhale. It's an intoxicating smell that makes me even harder. But that's not my goal either.

I grab hold of his thighs and lift his legs and hips, exposing his behind and opening it.

I salivate. The delicious line that I have admired so much is now before me. The strand of blond hair fills her in and swirls around the tight, slightly pink orifice.

My mouth is watering.

I reach over and lick it lightly. He lets out a strangled moan. I think he did not expect me to take this step. I don't think about it when I bury my head there. I'm hungry and I eat it. My tongue tries to enter while my lips salivate everything. Ben's spasms of pleasure excite me even more, and I devour him harder. So much so that I hear his voice.

"Stop it, man, or I cum."

I'm not done yet; you can't do that to me.

I pull away while I spit on my hand and lubricate my dick.

He bites his lip because he has understood what I mean.

I go up as I approach it, and I stop right at the entrance.

I kiss him, I caress him. I pinch his nipples. And when I stick my tongue down his throat, I squeeze and pierce the sphincter.

He groans. It's normal, I have a good prick. But I stop until the pain passes, and he nods between my lips.

I advance a little more, and a little more, and still a little more.

Once inside, I remain still, until he begins to move his hips.

I fuck him slowly, licking his mouth, biting his neck.

He moans in my arms, his legs wrapped around my waist. He covers my back with caresses, he pats my ass, which thrusts into him without pause, sometimes fast, other times so slow that he squirms with pleasure.

With our bodies pressed against each other, Ben lets out a moan so prolonged that it accompanies a jet of heat on my stomach.

At that moment, I am so aroused that with a single movement of my hip I empty myself inside him, while I let out the deepest moan of my life, and I am overwhelmed by a feeling of happiness that I did not know before.

# CHAPTER 12

We have stayed embraced in bed, in silence, not daring to say anything. Then we showered together, maintaining contact under the hot water with the same silent embrace.

I don't know what's going through his head, but mine is a whirlwind of emotions, sensations that have no answer. I love Sue, I love my girlfriend, and never before have I felt any attraction to another man. I'm sure of that. I'm a gym enthusiast, I've been seeing asses and dicks all my life, and I've never been struck by this desire, this need to touch him, to kiss him, to devour him.

I'm also an experienced guy in bed. Before Sue, many women have wet my sheets, and I'm demanding when it comes to sex. However, the fuck I just had with the new one, Ben, has been the most mind-blowing of my life. I don't know how long we've been together. Whether it was seconds or hours. It's as if we have transcended time and only the two of us, a bed, and this immense desire exist.

We dress in the same silence that has overwhelmed us since we screwed. Only then do I look at the clock. It's ten o'clock. A perfect time to go down for breakfast.

"Are you okay?" he asks me.

I don't know the answer. Let's just say the delicious fatigue that envelops us after coming still lingers, but I haven't fully accepted that I just fucked a guy, a friend, and had a great time.

"Let's go down for breakfast," I reply evasively. "I'm hungry."

We take the elevator together. I know he's sneaking glances at me, but he doesn't dare speak or approach me. I appreciate that because I have a lot to process, if I can even manage to do so.

The guys are already at a long table on the terrace, overlooking the snowy peaks.

"Sleepyheads!" Mark exclaims upon seeing us. "What the fuck have you two been up to?"

"Ben woke up with a hangover," I say, smiling at him, and he returns the smile.

"I'm doing pretty well considering the bender I got yesterday," he says, and everyone laughs and jokes. "No alcohol for me today. What are our plans?"

Mark explains that he will join us in the afternoon since he needs to stop by the agricultural fair. Edward has gotten ski passes for all of us, so we'll be skiing.

"What about the snow equipment?" Ben asks.

"We'll rent it. I'm sure they have your size."

More jokes, some coffee, and eggs with bacon. Suddenly, it's almost eleven, and we need to head up to the ski resort. Ben gets in the other car, not without giving me a long, intense look that sends shivers down my spine once again.

During the ascent, I can't stop thinking about him. About the taste of his skin, the silky resistance of his opening as my tongue tried to penetrate it, the delightful pressure of his sphincter welcoming my dick. I have to cross my legs and focus on the damn country music playing on the radio.

The afternoon flies by, and I hardly see him. We cross paths on the chairlifts, and when I descend, he's in the middle of a run. I'm having a good time, but I find myself searching for him among the crowd of brightly colored skiers on the slope.

It's almost dark when we finally gather at one of the bars in the ski resort, where Mark is already waiting for us with a couple of beers in his system.

"I've ordered a round," he greets us.

The bar is crowded with people who want to have a good time. But I only have eyes for Ben. When I saw him appear, wearing a thick cream wool sweater, washed jeans, and brown boots, I wanted to kiss him. His blond hair is tousled, and as he leans back in his chair to talk to Rubens, I notice a group of girls looking at him with bright eyes and whispering among themselves.

"I'm going to take a leak," I announce, and as I pass by him, I give his butt a light pinch.

He hides it well, as if nothing happened.

"I'll go with you. I'm about to burst," he says and follows me.

When we enter the restroom, I first make sure we're alone, and then I pounce on him and kiss him.

He receives me with a satisfied smile on those lips that I devour eagerly, sucking, biting, as if I need them to sustain myself.

"I haven't stopped thinking about you all day," he whispers in my ear, moaning.

He writhes against me, on top of me, and I can feel that he's excited.

Voices are heard, and we immediately separate, each taking a spot at the urinal.

Two guys who are speaking French enter. One uses the toilet, and the other takes the one that's free to my left. I hear the intruder's stream hitting the porcelain. I squeeze, and a strong jet comes out even though I just peed before entering the bar.

When we're alone again, I look at Ben. I get lost in his eyes. I'm dragged along by them.

He reaches out his hand and grabs my dick. I look down at his long, thick, strong fingers caressing the opening of the glans, while the last drops wet it, which, more than caring, seems to excite him. Meanwhile, he starts stroking himself slowly, masturbating in a way that's partially visible between his fingers.

"I want to go back to the room. Now. With you," he says, his eyes gleaming.

"We can't just leave like that. We'll have to wait," I say, although he doesn't like the idea. Voices are heard behind the door again. He withdraws his hand, but before he does, he gives me a light kiss on the lips.

Two more guys enter, and Ben bids me farewell with a gesture. When he leaves, I look at my dick. He managed to get me hard again, so I have to wait for it to go down before I put it away. Wait for it to go down and for this horniness to subside, because all I can think about now is what I'm going to do to him when I have him before me tonight, in the room.

# CHAPTER 13

As soon as the elevator door closes, we throw ourselves at each other and start kissing passionately. I slip my hand under his sweater to find that he's not wearing a shirt. I'm tempted to take it off right there and lick his nipples. I caress his warm, smooth skin, which feels comforting and arousing. He puts his hand inside my pants.

"I love your dick," he whispers in my ear before biting my earlobe.

The elevator stops. We're on our floor. We step out of it, still entangled, pressed against the opposite wall. I desire him so much that my balls ache. He goes further with his hand, trapped inside, and caresses them as if he can read my mind.

My glans has pushed through the boxer briefs and the waistband of my pants, slightly askew but close to my navel. A bit of precum has lubricated it, leaving a stain on the fabric edge. Ben notices and moans. Right there, in the middle of the hallway, he gets down on his knees and licks that part, taking large licks, swallowing the remnants of seminal fluid.

I look both ways. Anyone could come out of their room and catch us, and it would be difficult to explain.

"Let's go to bed," I whisper, my voice filled with desire.

Ben finishes licking, but eventually gets up, kisses me, holds the front of my pants, fully aware that the back of his fingers is brushing against my dick, and pulls me toward the end of the hallway.

Desire makes my hands tremble, but in the end, I manage to use the magnetic key card, and the door opens. We rush into the room, falling onto the bed. I lie on my back, and he lies on top of me.

The kisses continue until Ben breaks away to take off his shirt. I do the same, never taking my eyes off him. Those eyes are magnetic to me.

Once free, he doesn't return to my mouth, but goes for my neck. I feel his mouth sucking, nibbling the spots beneath my jawline, then kissing and caressing them.

He descends along my collarbone, and his tongue entangles itself in the tangle of my chest hair.

"I like that you're hairy," he says, pulling on a few strands while nibbling my nipples.

I don't know what it is about that mouth, but an electric current runs through me, even though I've never been particularly sensitive in that area. While he toys with one of my nipples, his long fingers play with the other. I arch my back, overcome with pleasure. I want to tell him to stop. To keep going. To shout at him. But in the end, he discovers something new and descends further.

He separates from me for a moment, sitting astride my thighs, and pulls my belt until it's undone. He does the same with my pants, and gently pulls down the white boxer briefs.

My dick appears fully erect and slaps against my abdomen a couple of times.

"Did I tell you how much I love your dick?" he repeats.

His eyes shine as he takes it into his mouth.

I lift my head to watch how he does it, how he engulfs it, while he never takes his eyes off mine.

That vision makes my fingers tingle. The way his tongue runs through it, the way hir lips kiss it, and hide it, until it disappears in his mouth. The way he chokes and looks like he's about to vomit. I hold his head in that position. The pleasure is unspeakable, because I feel my dick stuck there, in his throat. He gags, but squeezes harder. In the end, I quit because I can cum, and that's still not my intention.

Ben breaks away and stands up, to remove what is left of his clothes. I take advantage and take off my pants and socks. The two naked. Me, lying on the bed. He, standing right in front.

"That body drives me crazy," he tells me, then bites his bottom lip.

I expect him to carry on with his work, with that giddy blowjob he was giving me, but instead he comes to bed, albeit in a different way.

We're both lying on our sides, his head is level with my genitals, so his...are level with my mouth.

Without further ado, he continues with the fabulous blowjob, calmer, enjoying what he's eating, with long licks, or light kisses all along the length of the dick.

I look at what I have in front of me. Ben has a nice dick. She is fat and big. With white skin and uncircumcised. There are a couple of swollen veins giving it a knobby appearance, and the glans appears lightly covered with skin at the base. He is also wet. The precum has left his juicy.

It's the second time in my life that I've been so close to a dick, and the first was this very morning, and this morning.

I put my nose close and sniff it. I recognize the smell of my underwear when I play sports. It is an acid aroma, juicy and full of sensuality. I've also smelled it in the gym when someone has taken a shower.

I reach out my hand and caress it. It throbs, and I feel it vibrate between my fingers. I kiss him. The skin is soft, more than I imagined, and with a warm touch. I realize that Ben has stopped and is looking at me.

"Pass your tongue," he tells me.

I listen to him and, somewhat awkwardly, pass it around the glans. It is an acid taste, like yogurt, but pleasant. I play with the tip of my tongue over the rounded shapes, and down to that swollen vein.

"Put it in your mouth," he orders me.

I do. The salty feeling increases. I realize that it turns me on. And when Ben continues to give him head, I forget about everything and do the same.

It's very different from eating a pussy. Here everything is firm, seasoned with the fluids that escape from the opening. I am learning as I practice. I know I'm not doing it right, that I'm letting Ben down, but I'm trying my best. I put it in as far as I can without it causing me to gag, I go out and go in. I lick it, nibble the tip and the trunk...

With a move I don't expect, Ben rolls me onto my back again, and he is on top of me. He adjusts until I get it in my mouth and begins to move, up and down.

I'm immobilized and he knows it. And he's fucking my mouth, faster and faster.

I try to take a breath, which I barely manage. His dick moves in and out of my lips, faster and faster. I grab onto his buttocks as I try to keep up, but he drives in so far that I gags.

I cough, but he doesn't stop. Neither does he stop with the generous blowjob he is giving me.

My vision blurs. Pleasure is something I don't remember ever feeling before. He caresses my balls while he sucks me, or masturbates me, or sticks it down his throat.

I'm about to come when Ben squeezes a little harder and he pushes me so far inside that he digs his nails into his buttocks.

And then he cums.

In my mouth.

Inside my trachea.

A generous cumshot that, when separated, escapes from the corner of my lips.

The sour, sweet, salty taste envelops me, while a stream of cum shoots out of my dick straight into his mouth.

He pulls it out to let me breathe as the last spasms of pleasure course through me.

Completely exhausted, with a stream of spunk running down my cheek, I try to recover, while Ben continues to suck me, despite having come, because he is still hungry for me.

71

# CHAPTER 14

We didn't fall asleep until dawn.

After each skirmish, we rested embraced and naked, sweaty, still trembling with pleasure. But soon the caresses, soft kisses began again, and desire nested in us, making us surrender to each other and return to the fray with even more eagerness for sex, for skin, for new games, and more pleasure.

During those intervals when we regained our strength, lying next to each other, we also talked. I learned that Ben is from Monroe, near Seattle, that he has two brothers, a high school swimming medal, and he cried his eyes out when his dog, Bendito, was run over by a car.

I feel so comfortable, so relaxed, that I share a bit about myself, something I don't usually do with the girls I date. Not even Sue, with whom I feel comfortable, knows so much about me. I explain why I like fishing, what I'm passionate about in athletics, and how I used to be a chubby kid who was teased by everyone.

"The only thing that's still fat is your dick," he says, shaking it with one hand and making me laugh.

He also tells me that he met Sharon at his best friend's bachelor party a couple of years ago. They met, joked around, had a tequila competition, and exchanged phone numbers. That fills me with confusion, so much so that I dare to ask.

"How long have you been doing this?"

"Do what?" he asks, not understanding.

I shrug. "It's obvious that I'm not the first."

"You are the first," he declares, surprised.

A cynical smile spreads across my face. How do I explain that nobody sucks a dick the way he does without any previous experience? I decide to explain it with a graphic image.

"My dick penetrated you like butter."

He smiles and runs a hand through his hair. He also bites his lower lip, making me desire him again.

"I mean..." he clarifies, "I've been with some guys, yes. The first one was that best friend with whom we went to a bachelor party, and I think that's where it all started."

"Do you still see each other?"

"We were teammates on the swim team. You know, hormones during adolescence, late-night training, showers..., what can I tell you?"

"So, you catch your victims in the showers too." He caught me in one of those.

He rests his head on my chest and plays with the curly hair on my pubic area.

"I think we almost had a relationship, even though he was still with his girlfriend, and I was with the girls I hooked up with on weekends," he pauses. "I don't know. It was weird. Even after he got married, he would call me sometimes and come over."

"To fuck."

He bursts into laughter.

"To fuck. He was the only one with whom I had that strange relationship. The others... just a horniness with someone who happened to be there at that moment."

I understand that he has led a life in which he has been with both guys and girls. I met a bartender at a bar in the South who claimed to fall in love with people, not bodies. But Ben only talks to me about sex.

"Since you've been with Sharon..." I hesitate to finish the sentence.

"Only once," he confesses. "I had to go back to Seattle to take an exam. After studying so much, I needed to blow off some steam, and... well, a guy hit on me and we did it in a public park."

A pang of jealousy hits me, but also desire. I imagine Ben with another man, outdoors, exposed to the gaze of others, and I feel my mouth go dry.

"And have you never thought about telling her?" I ask him. "About this."

He sighs. Maybe I'm going too far with the questioning. He rests his head on his hand and looks me in the eyes.

"Dozens, hundreds, thousands of times, but when I was about to do it, I thought it was just once, a heat-of-the-moment thing due to excessive stress, that many guys cheat on their wives or girlfriends with others, and I wouldn't be doing anything different."

I know about the adventures of most of my friends. Almost all of them, as Ben says, have cheated on their wives or girlfriends at some point, and they all find excuses: being drunk, unable to stop, not remembering anything until they woke up in someone else's bed.

I'm not one to judge anyone, but I have never cheated on a girl I've been in a relationship with. If I've desired someone else, I've ended the relationship..., except now.

"And what about you?" Ben asks me, surely noticing that I can't stop thinking about what we're doing. "Have you ever been with a guy?"

"Never," I reply without hesitation.

"And you've never thought about it?"

"Never."

He bites my collarbone and leans on top of me.

"Oh, come on! With how attractive you are, someone must have tried."

I shrug.

"Yes, maybe once, but I made it clear that I'm into girls."

He adjusts to my body. I love how he does it, because it feels like every part of his anatomy fits perfectly with mine.

"The tough guy that all the queers in this town have jerked off to," he says dreamily, referring to me.

"Don't say things like that," I feel a bit shy.

"I guarantee it," he winks at me. "You have an irresistible appeal. I liked you a lot even before I met you when they showed me pictures of the team you were on. I thought, 'Who's that hunk?'"

"Well, what a disappointment when you met me."

He smiles.

"When I met you, my mouth was watering. I had the best jerk-off sessions since my adolescence, all while thinking about you."

I get nervous. I give him a kiss on the cheek and push him off me. Now it's me who leans on my elbow to look him in the eyes.

"Changing the subject..." I react. "So, in your case, I shouldn't be the first, as you told me earlier."

He protests, furrowing his eyebrows.

"You are the first."

"And what about your high school buddy? And the guy in the park?"

"I only fucked them," he pauses briefly. "With you, I think I've fallen in love."

Something runs down my spine. The damn confusion comes back. This is just a weekend fling, and it's already complicated enough. How can love be involved in this shit?

"Don't talk nonsense," I say, feeling uncomfortable.

He smiles and settles back on top of me. He handles my body wonderfully. He knows where and when to touch. He slightly spreads his legs and, reaching out his arm, he places my dick, which is ready again, in that tight area where the anus meets the base of the testicles.

"And now I would like you to fuck me."

He moves just enough for me to feel the pressure, his mouth slightly opening, the movement of his hips.

"Why do you turn me on so much?" I ask, my voice filled with desire.

"Because you and I are destined to be together."

# CHAPTER 15

We go down late for breakfast. A cold shower managed to separate me from him, but the dark circles reflected in the bathroom mirror can't be fixed with cold water.

Ben left the room earlier, to avoid suspicion. When I arrive, everyone is already there, and breakfast is almost over. I take the only available chair next to Mark.

"What are the plans for today?" I ask.

"We'll hang out at bars. We have to go back by noon," he replies.

I sense a hint of dryness in his tone, but I suppose the sales at the fair haven't been as good as they should be. He's a good salesman, but if he's with his buddies instead of at the booth where his clients are...

I'm hungry and I devour what's left on the plates.

"It's like you haven't eaten in a year, dude," Edward comments.

From the other end of the table, Ben winks at me discreetly. I need to gather strength, because I still intend to find a moment before we leave to have one last encounter with him. Even if it's in a public garden.

When we leave the hotel to have coffee with beer at the highest point of the town, Mark holds me back, gripping my arm.

"Can we talk for a moment?" he asks.

I look at him strangely. He's the type of guy you can't talk to in private because he always delivers his messages to the collective. I don't think I've ever seen him without being surrounded by friends all these years.

"Yes, of course," I reply.

He waits until everyone goes ahead, and only then does he speak.

"What the hell are you doing?"

I don't know what he's referring to.

"I have no idea what you're talking about."

"About Ben."

A wave of fear runs through my spine.

"What about Ben?" I ask defensively.

He looks around and lowers his voice. His face is red, and he seems very upset.

"I saw you last night. I went upstairs to ask you for something for my headache, and I saw you in the hallway."

The image of what we did there comes to my mind, as if it were a projection. Kisses, caresses, a blowjob, and many words that sounded like sex. I try to confuse him.

"I don't know what you thought you saw."

"I saw him giving you a blowjob."

So, he saw it. I knew we were exposed, that anyone coming out of their room would encounter that, but I couldn't imagine it would be one of my best friends.

"The hallway was dark, and we were all drunk," I try to make him believe he saw something else. "I was just trying to help him get up. Nothing more."

He pauses, expecting me to do the same. He's upset, and could lose his composure in front of the others who just turned the corner and are out of sight.

"I saw you kissing each other," he says as if it were a condemnation, "and I saw him dragging you into the room."

He's very clear about what he saw, and he won't change his mind. We've committed an indiscretion, and we've been caught. I'm scared, I admit it. I've embarked on this without knowing what I'm doing. But today, this morning, all I can think about is Ben and how these hours together, sweaty and happy, have been, how for the first time, I've felt like myself.

"Don't get involved in this," I warn him.

"And then I stayed outside the door, listening," Mark continues. "And I heard you fucking. Fucking, man."

I feel violated when I should feel embarrassed. It's as if he had been recording our intimacy. An act that belongs only to Ben and me, and Mark has insisted on... I still don't know what.

I decide it's best to let it go for a few days. That way, I'll have time to think about what the hell I've gotten myself into, what the hell I'm going to do, and what explanations I'm going to give Mark.

"It's not the right time to talk about this."

"I know you, Jacob," but he's not willing to stop, "and I know this shit isn't your thing. So, drop it, and drop it now. Right now. Before we go back to town."

That pisses me off. Yes, I'm cheating on Sue. Yes, I'm fucking a guy. But he has no right to tell me what to do.

"And what if I don't want to?" it comes out of my mouth.

Mark analyzes me. I don't think I'm reacting the way he expected. Maybe he thought I would cower? That I would apologize? He looks at me with an unfriendly expression and thumps my chest with his thumb.

"I'll have to tell the guys. I don't want people like that on the team. And Sue, of course."

A threat. A clear threat.

"And what are you going to do with Ben?"

"He's out," he grits his teeth. "I don't know how the hell I didn't see it coming. I have an eye for guys like him. I'll come up with an excuse that won't compromise you, but we won't see him again starting today."

"Are you going to tell Sharon too?"

I'm curious to know how far he intends to go.

"If necessary, yes. But I hope he has some ounce of manhood left and tells her himself."

The last sentence makes my blood boil. Ben is more of a man than him and many of those who boast about their conquests in great detail.

I can't contain myself and I punch him. It was instinctive, as if a spring had been pressed, and... surprise!

But I don't regret it when I see him on the ground, touching his chin with a look of astonishment.

"Ben is more of a man than you," I say and spit, "And I'll do whatever I want, whenever I want."

And without further ado, I leave him lying there as I join the band.

# CHAPTER 16

The return has been strange. My mind hasn't traveled with my companions, but in the other car, where Ben and Mark were, imagining terrible things.

We arrived first. The other vehicle disappeared from sight a while ago, which still gives me an uncomfortable feeling in my stomach.

My house is empty. Sue has keys, but today we had agreed not to see each other. I told her shortly after we met that trips with the guys require some recovery time. That the liver and the head need to heal.

I try to do something. A house always has something to fix, but I leave everything halfway. I pace around the living room like a caged wolf, enter my room, and lie down on the bed, only to get up again and resume pacing up and down.

In the end, I grab a beer and sit in the porch rocking chair, trying to make sense of everything that has happened. I could summarize it as having had sex with a man, a man I met at the gym, that I had a great time, and that my best friend is determined to get rid of him.

And that should be it.

It should all stay there: a torrid affair, a period of time where, without realizing it, I was so hot that I had no scruples about where to put it.

Two things are clear to me: I'm not a fag, and this has only been a lapse in my life.

However, there's something else. And that something is constantly spinning in my head, scratching my heart and driving me crazy.

It's nighttime when, without thinking twice, I grab the car keys and decide to do it.

Between what he has told me and what I've heard the guys say about it, I know where he lives. I drive with a bitter knot in my throat and the absolute conviction that I'm making a mistake.

I park on the back street and make my way through the community gardens, taking refuge in the shadows cast by the streetlights under the trees.

This must be it. It's a modest house, painted white, with a flowerbed planted next to the door. There's a window, the curtains undrawn, and I see Sharon preparing something in the kitchen in the background. Ben is there too. The lamp that turns on under his eyes leaves him in the shadows, and he seems very focused, with a thick book open, taking notes in a notebook.

I hold my breath to calm myself. I'm wearing the hood of my sweatshirt, so they can't recognize me. I fidget anxiously next to the door. The street is quiet, only the distant barking of a dog can be heard.

Finally, I knock with my knuckles a couple of times on the sturdy wood.

"Are you going?" I hear Sharon's voice from a distance.

I feel my breath stop. It's as if I have a buzzing sound in my ears. Seconds pass, and finally the door opens.

Ben is there, looking at me with surprised eyes. He's wearing very loose sweatpants and an old Lakers t-shirt. There's a moment of silence where neither of us does anything. He looks back as if he wants to check if his girl is realizing how strange this situation is. But Sharon seems to have forgotten about the visit and continues manipulating a steaming pot.

"Jacob, it's great to see you here," he exclaims loud enough for her to hear.

Now it's Sharon's turn to turn and greet me with a wave. I respond and speak in a low voice.

"Did the return trip go well?"

Ben is so puzzled that I notice him keeping some distance.

"Boring," he shrugs.

"Did Mark say anything to you?"

"He wouldn't stop talking."

I bite my lower lip, a gesture I can't suppress when I'm impatient. I see his eyes darting there, and he swallows hard.

"I'm referring to something between us," I clarify in a very low voice.

He looks back again. His girl continues cooking, unaware of what we're up to.

"Between us?" His voice carries a hint of alarm. "What does he know?"

"He saw us in the hallway."

He looks at me, surprised. There's worry in those gray eyes that I can't stop staring at. His blond hair is disheveled, as if he had been playing with it while focusing on his books. Finally, he swallows hard and crosses his arms.

"Did he tell you what he's going to do?" he asks me, and I shrug.

"He'll find a moment to talk to you. He'll kick you off the team, and if we see each other again, he'll spill the beans."

He runs a hand over his mouth and looks back at Sharon, still oblivious to the brewing storm. When he looks at me again, he comes close enough to speak into my ear. Close enough for me to smell his cologne, faded amidst the salty and robust scent of his sweat. He takes a moment to speak, and when he does, his voice sounds more guttural.

"I'm not going to stop seeing you..." He steps back and looks into my eyes, "...unless you..."

I remain motionless, by the door, hands in my pockets, my face partially hidden by the hood.

"Step out for a moment," he says, sounding like an order, although that wasn't my intention.

He seems confused. He doesn't understand anything, and he must be scared.

"Honey," he turns around, "I'll be right back."

She raises her hand but doesn't even look at us. A ridiculous thought crosses my mind that I would like to taste a dish made with such devotion.

Finally, he closes the door behind him and stands there expectantly. I start walking. He follows me, but we don't speak. I take the first alley to the right. It's a narrow gap between the backyards of two houses, barely a meter wide, filled with dirty soil and darkness.

I stop when I'm sure no one can see us. Ben does the same behind me.

And then I grab him tightly by the collar of his hoodie and push him against the wall. He looks at me with wide eyes, but his surprise doesn't last long because my next move is to dive into his mouth.

I desire him so much that I kiss him with fury, with hunger, almost with hatred. He breathes, unevenly, between my lips, pushes back my hood, and tangles his fingers in my hair.

My body against his seems to want to merge with him, my hips thrusting, seeking, while my hands roam his skin over the fabric, thirsty for the touch they still remember.

"Jacob," he moans as I nibble beneath his earlobe.

I forcefully pull down his old sweatpants, which end up around his ankles, tangled like a bunch of green leaves. He's not wearing underwear, so I'm met with his swollen, thick dick, moving involuntarily with pleasure-driven motions.

I take it in hand and begin to masturbate him while not stopping the kiss.

"Jacob," he moans again between my lips.

With the other hand, I unbuckle my belt, delve into my pants, and pull mine out, smearing my fingers with slick and liquid precum.

He tries to grab it, but I don't let him. I push him back with my torso, immobilize him with my shoulders, and with both hands, slightly parting our hips, I grasp the two dicks, pressed tightly together, simulating the wet crevice I enjoy so much in Ben.

He understands what I intend and starts moving, while I synchronize my hips with his, never ceasing our kisses.

I glance down, the two glandes, joined by the area where the incision progresses, appear and disappear between my fingers, fused together, exchanging heat.

I accelerate the motion for him to follow.

He moans once again into my mouth.

"I'm going to come."

I don't respond, because at that moment the jet of cum spurts from my dick, splashing our bellies, while my throat stifles a moan between his lips.

That makes it even more intense, so Ben fulfills what he said, and before the final spasms of milk come from my dick, he releases the first ones. A thick, hot stream reaches heights, drenching my hoodie and ends up shooting between my fingers.

Moaning, we remain with our foreheads pressed together as we try to recover from the orgasm.

"What are we going to do?" he asks me.

I don't answer and, without saying a word, while I fasten my pants, I leave there, heading to my car.

# CHAPTER 17

Sue called me a couple of times this morning, but I didn't answer the phone. At work, my boss asked if I was okay. The bastard seems to have a radar for his employees, that's how well his business works. I must not look good. Tonight, I haven't slept a wink thinking about how to handle all of this.

When I finish work, I go straight to Sue's house. She's wallpapering the inside of an old piece of furniture she wants to give me. It's a dresser she found in a dumpster and has been restoring in her free time.

She wraps her arms around my neck and kisses me.

"I missed you."

It doesn't take her long to realize that something is wrong. I must look more serious than usual, or maybe I'm not doing what I usually do: taking her to bed. The sex between us has always been good. Until Ben.

"We need to talk," I pronounce the phrase, and at the same time I curse myself for using such a hackneyed formula.

My tone, or my face, tell her that it's something serious. She steps back, crosses her arms, and looks at me with her head slightly raised, as if she needs to defend herself from me.

"Has something happened?"

"Yes."

Her eyes stare at mine. She wants to be prepared for what's coming because she knows it's going to hurt.

"During that fucking trip you've taken?"

"That's right."

She swallows and changes her posture.

"You've been with someone else."

I came here for this, so I have to face it.

"Yes, I've been with someone else."

She holds back the tears and covers her mouth so I can't see how much it hurts her. I won't say it because she'll call me "opportunistic" and won't believe me, but taking this step is hurting me as much as it is hurting her.

"I thought what we had..." She can't finish the sentence.

"I did too. I was sure."

Suddenly, I see a glimmer of understanding in her eyes. It's as if she's reconsidering and giving a new interpretation to what I just told her.

"Was it just a fling? Are you here to ask for forgiveness?"

I let out a sigh. It's already difficult enough not to be clear.

"I have no idea what it was, but I need time to figure it out."

She shrugs slightly, although her arms remain crossed.

"If it was just a heat-of-the-moment thing... I could forgive you."

I feel like hugging her. I know she loves me, but now I realize how much. She would be willing to endure infidelity just to keep us together.

"It made me reconsider many things." My hands in my pockets, because I don't know what to do with them. "I can't continue with you without being clear about who I am and what I want."

Her gaze sharpens. Sue is smart, and she's connecting every sentence, every thought, and something doesn't add up for her.

"What aren't you telling me?"

I fidget where I stand. Until this very moment, I haven't verbalized it. Doing it in front of the person I had decided to share my life with is especially painful.

"I've slept with a man," I confess.

She looks at me as if I just said that everything before was a joke.

"I don't believe you."

"Do you think I would tell you something like this if it weren't true?"

She studies me again. She knows me well. It doesn't take much time to get to know someone, just a good intuition.

"With whom," she tightens her arms.

"With one of your…friends?"

I lower my head. I knew it was going to be hard, but I'm not going to blurt out Ben's name. That is something for him to decide for himself.

"Sue, don't insist."

She comes over to me, and with a hand on my chin he forces me to look at her.

"As a teenager, I also spent a night with one of my friends, and it meant nothing." ·

"This has been different."

Her forehead wrinkles. Her gaze turns questioning.

"You're telling me that you liked it. More than when you are with me."

I'm not going to tell him that fucking Ben was the most delicious thing I've ever done.

"I need time to understand what is happening to me and to be able to make a decision. I wanted you to know. I wanted to be honest with you. I am not one of those who deceive the people they love."

She nods and she turns away. She takes a walk around the room. She is so shrunken in on herself that she seems smaller. She stops to look at me again.

"Since when do you know?"

"What?"

"That you like men."

She released the air contained in her lungs.

"I've never been attracted to them."

"It's not possible." She has raised her voice more than she wants, because she continues to lower it so much that it's hard for me to hear her. Those things don't happen overnight.

"Sue," I try to make her understand, "if I had any other answer than the one I gave you, I would tell you. I want nothing. I don't ask you for anything. I just wanted you to know it.

She nods and heads to the kitchen area. For a moment I think she's going to take one of those butcher knives and stab me ten times, but she only fills a glass of water, to the brim, and she drinks it all.

From where she is, across the living room from the kitchen, she asks me again.

"What will we tell the others? They will ask. They always ask what happened."

I know. This afternoon. Or tomorrow when they see her taciturn. Or at the next meeting, when Sue doesn't show up.

"What do you want us to tell them?" I ask her, because I think it is her right to make that decision.

She looks me up and down.

"That they've broken your ass and now you like being fucked from behind..." —but she smiles, and for a moment I see tenderness in her eyes—, "but we'll tell them that we don't have the same goals. It's something I hear lately in the movies."

I nod. I know you don't understand me, but at no time have I doubted that you would not use this information to attack me.

I have nothing more to say, and I don't want to add empty words either which end up spoiling it. I turn on my way to the exit.

"Jacob," she calls me.

With her hand already on the door, I turn to her.

"Be careful." —Yes, there is tenderness in her eyes—. "I don't know who this man is, but he looks like this is going to be painful for you."

95

# CHAPTER 18

My next visit is to Mark's house.

His wife tells me he's in the backyard, chopping wood for the winter.

I go around the house and find him there, sweaty, with an axe in his hand and a pile of logs forming a mountain.

As soon as he sees me, he puffs up his chest, adopts that gruff look that can be intimidating, but he doesn't say anything.

I walk slowly across the well-kept lawn, untouched by frost, until I stop right in front of him. We hold each other's gaze. I know he's measuring what he's going to do, so I clear things up for him.

"I've come to ask for your forgiveness," I blurt out.

He squints his eyes and remains silent for a few seconds, but his shoulders relax, and he tosses the axe to the side.

"A beer?" he asks me, already grabbing two from the ice-filled fridge resting on a bench.

He uncorks them open and hands one to me. The first sip makes me realize how thirsty I am. I don't think I've had a drink all day. We sit, one on each side of the white cork fridge, as if it were an arbitrator. We drink without talking, looking ahead, at nothing, trying to mend our friendship.

I've known Mark since I arrived in this town. He was the first to speak to me, the first to have a beer like this with me, the first to whom I confided that I liked Sue.

"I'm glad you've come to your senses," he says after a long while, raising his bottle as if it were an achievement. "We all have a strange moment in life. Once I got into casinos. It lasted a couple of months, but all I could think about was playing roulette. As quickly as it came, it went away, leaving my bank account nearly empty."

I turn my head to look him in the eyes. I want him to understand what I'm about to say.

"I don't regret what I've done, Mark. It scares me, I don't understand it, and it's hard for me to recognize myself, but I don't regret it."

He furrows his brow, annoyed.

"I know you. That's not like you."

"I'm not like what?"

"You're not into that stuff."

"Because you know it. You're sure."

He looks away from me and loses himself again in some indeterminate place within the confines of his garden. "Nobody knows anybody," the saying goes, and that should be reason enough to end our conversation.

"I also need to apologize to you," he declares, but still without looking at me. "I lost my mind when I saw you two... doing that. It's not up to me to decide for you."

More silence.

Sometimes, things happen between us where words are unnecessary. We can spend an entire afternoon without uttering a single one and still feel as close as if we had revealed our deepest intimacies.

"I just told Sue," I blurt out.

The surprise in his eyes tells me it's something he didn't expect.

"What did she say?"

"She's as shocked as you and I are."

He nods.

"Have you broken up?"

I take a long sip. At some point in the past few weeks, I came to the conclusion that Sue was the one. I like her, we get along well, I think about her often, and she respects this silence of mine that has annoyed many others. Perhaps that's why I've made the decision.

"I can't continue with her after what happened."

"Yes, you can," he says. He gestures for another beer, as mine is nearly empty, but I decline. "Years ago, I had an affair. A coworker. It lasted too long, to the point where I had to decide where I wanted to be. I told Anne about it. We went through a rough patch. She still throws it in my face when she's angry. But here we are."

I raise an eyebrow. He's answered his own question.

"But you chose Anne."

He looks at me without understanding, until I see in his eyes that he has just grasped the meaning of my words.

"Does that mean... you've chosen Ben?"

Ben, who has turned my world upside down in two weeks.

"I don't think we'll be intimate again. Right now, I need to be alone."

"Then what?"

That "then" hasn't left my mind since the first time I saw Ben's ass and thought about how comfortable it would be to be there.

I take the last sip and leave the bottle in the fridge. I stand up. I've fulfilled the purpose for which I came.

"I have to figure out who I am so I don't deceive myself and others."

Mark also stands up and extends his hand. This is the friend I knew. I shake it. He grips tightly, and I realize how much I needed it.

"Thanks for telling me," he says when we part. "It's strange, but thanks for trusting me."

I nod. He and I have never smiled at each other. That would be too soft. Before I leave, I ask him the other question that brought me here.

"What will you do about Ben? Have you kicked him off the team?"

He crosses his arms, and his face takes on a mocking expression that I know well.

"I decided not to do anything while we were coming back from Black Mountain. He's a good guy. Whether he scores the goal or gets scored on... that's up to him."

I nod. I'm grateful for that. Let Ben do whatever he wants when he deems it appropriate, but let others not make decisions for him.

"I have to go," I reply. My eyes ache from lack of sleep. "I need to get some rest."

He raises a hand in farewell.

"And, you bastard," he says before I leave, touching his jaw, "you should have competed in boxing. You have a right hook that packs a punch."

# CHAPTER 19

There's one more thing I need to do.

I'm nervous and uncomfortable, but I want to understand what the hell is happening to me, so I can make a decision.

I quickly have dinner while fiddling with the computer, searching for the coordinates. I throw the plate into the sink and step into the shower. I need to clear my mind and feel clean. When I come out of the bathroom, I rummage through the wardrobe. Worn-out jeans and a black t-shirt seem fine. There's not much to choose from anyway. As I close the wardrobe door, the mirror reflects my naked image, and I pause for a moment, looking at myself.

There's very little fat on this body, and a lifetime dedicated to sports, to my passion, has defined each of those muscles: the breadth of my pecs, the volume of my arms, the density of my thighs, and this flat and hairy belly with a narrow waist that widens my back even more.

I also look at my dick. I know it's big, and not just because Ben says so. It's inevitable for guys to compare them at the gym, stealing furtive glances to see how well-endowed this or that buddy is. It's dark, with pronounced veins, and the head slightly peeking out of the foreskin, which naturally retracts a bit. It's incredible how it dilates when I get aroused, how it grows, and the tension those veins reach, hard like ropes.

I look away and finish getting dressed. I've searched for the address on the Internet, and it's an hour's drive away.

I drive at a good speed, with country music playing and the window rolled down. It's a way to connect with myself and also relax.

When I enter the city, filled with blinking lights, I realize how isolated we are in our town, how small we are, how disconnected from this urban and sparkling atmosphere.

I drive through the deserted streets of the suburbs until I reach the city center. Just by turning a corner, the silence breaks, the solitude disappears, and the streets are filled with people eager to have fun, with open restaurants and crowded terrace bars.

I'm lucky and find parking. Mark says you have to touch your balls to find one, and I assure you it's true.

I get out of the car and look around. The GPS says it's two blocks away. I walk quickly, searching for the sign. A group of girls wearing heart-shaped headbands asks me if I want to join them. I politely dodge them with a smile and continue on my way.

I see the illuminated sign across the street, Burlesque, and head towards it with a certain unease in my stomach.

There are a couple of guys at the door. One seems to be the bouncer, the other wears false eyelashes and a sequin top. The first one looks me up and down and asks for twenty dollars to enter. I rummage through my wallet, but the other guy gently stops my hand.

"You can go in for free. I'm sure more than one will thank me for it."

I thank him as well and finally enter.

When he opens the red-painted door, the sound of electronic music slaps me in the face. There's a long and steep staircase descending. I hesitate for a moment. Eventually, I go down, heart racing, and my pupils trying to adjust to the strobe lights.

A spotlight blinds me for a moment, and when I can finally focus, I find myself in a large room with low ceilings, packed with men. They come in all types and ages, and most of them are dancing on the dance floor, swaying to the hypnotic bass.

A couple of them are making out a few steps away from me. Another person is hugging a shirtless guy from behind. Their hand is inside the pants, and by the movement, they're masturbating him.

I feel like a weirdo. All of this is so foreign to me, so strange, that I barely knew it existed a few hours ago, when I decided to search on the Internet for gay venues in the nearest city.

I need a drink, and I see the bar in the back. I make my way there, dodging suggestive glances that follow me along the way. There's only one bartender and a lot of people ordering drinks. I stay in a corner, not sure what to do. From there, I can discover the nuanced aspects of this world that I never imagined would intersect with my life.

"If you stay there, they'll never serve you," a voice states.

I look towards the voice. Right beside me, there's a guy observing me with a nice smile on his lips and his arms crossed. He's quite young, very blond, with a hoop earring on one ear and a wide, brightly colored shirt.

"And what should I do?" I try to make myself heard over the music.

"What do you drink?"

"Bourbon."

Mocking grimace.

"That's macho stuff."

"What should I drink then?"

"Bourbon," he winks at me. "Wait here. Don't go with anyone."

I find it amusing, especially when I see him walk away to the center of the bar, greeting people and making his way to the bartender. He quickly returns with two drinks, handing one to me.

"I've never seen you around the scene," he says.

I'm not quite sure what he means.

"It's my first time here."

He looks me up and down, though his gaze lingers briefly between my knees and my navel.

"Are you from the city?"

"No."

He smiles and raises his glass.

"To handsome outsiders."

I'm not used to being called that, and I don't mean "outsider." In the world I come from, it's me who says it to a girl, and rarely.

"To you," I also raise my glass.

I take a sip that burns my throat, but it feels great, because it helps calm my nerves. They just started playing a song that must be very popular, because it receives a general cheer, but I've never heard it in my life.

The guy leans in, resting his elbows on the empty space of the bar next to me.

"What's your plan for tonight?" he asks.

I could answer anything, but I know what I came here for, and this guy is friendly and quite attractive.

"I intend to find someone and search for a hotel."

When he looks at me, his eyes sparkle.

"I like that plan. What kind of person are you looking for?"

I lean in just enough to whisper it in his ear. My beard brushes against his smooth neck, and I feel him suppress a moan.

"Someone like you."

I step back to see his expression. He bites his lips and does the same as I did. He gets close to whisper in my ear, and I feel the contact of his smooth cheek against my earlobe.

"I'd love to go with you," he claims, looking into my eyes, "but I have a boyfriend."

Suddenly, I realize I've acted like a kid. I assumed... I assumed that his kindness...

"I'm sorry if I offended you," I plead, placing a hand over my heart.

He smiles.

"And my boyfriend and I," he looks me up and down, "do everything together. Would you be open to having both of us in that hotel room? I promise you'll have a good time."

My expression of dismay transforms into a conspiratorial look. I've had a great time with two women in bed. How will it be with two men?

"Who is he?" I ask.

He points to another guy, also quite young, with long, black hair and tanned skin. He has a bit of a rogue, ethnic air. He wears an open shirt and shows off a slim yet muscular body. He's observing me from a distance, in the middle of the dance floor, as if he knows what we're talking about.

I drink the bourbon in one gulp.

"That sounds good to me."

The guy gives me a light kiss on the lips and grabs my arm.

"Well, you're going to save on the hotel, because you're coming to our house."

"That would be even better."

The dark-haired guy is already approaching us.

There's something very virile about him that is attractive, perhaps the confidence with which he keeps analyzing me.

When he reaches my side, he extends his hand.

"Good choice," I'm not sure if he's saying it to me or to his boyfriend.

I shake his hand; the touch is warm, firm. I like it. I understand that they do this often, looking for someone to have a threesome with, because he seems to know how it works, and they haven't even spoken.

"Let's have a couple of drinks, dance, and then..." he says.

He has a deep, guttural voice.

"I don't know how to dance," I confess.

He looks at me seriously, until his mouth twists into a smile.

"Just this drink, and then we'll go home. I like you too much to waste the night."

# CHAPTER 20

It's a tiny apartment where the kitchen, living room and bedroom are all the same space. It's right above a bar, so the music's noise seems to penetrate through the walls and throb like a heartbeat. However, it's pleasant, with a large window that reflects the colors of the neon lights outside and retro furniture that shuns formality.

The bed is in a corner under the window, adorned with cushions to resemble a sofa.

Along the way, we've already done a few things. The dark-haired guy kissed me in a corner, and the blond one slipped his hand inside my pants, supposedly to see what he's in for.

"Damn!" he exclaimed. "I'm not sure if that's going to fit."

But his expression says otherwise.

We've climbed the stairs in a whirlwind of kisses and embraces. Of caresses. Of hands seeking and finding.

Once inside, they leave me alone for a few seconds and turn on a table lamp that casts a dim light, along with some candles on the surfaces of the furniture. I remain expectant, watching them, preparing everything for a session of sex with a stranger.

It's the blond one who approaches me. I recognize that he's handsome and has a seductive smile. He slowly approaches, until his body presses against mine and, very slowly, he starts kissing me. He does it well. His lips nibble at the corner of my mouth, his tongue entwines and then licks me, while he uses his chin to stroke my cheek when he pulls away.

I feel the other body behind me. Very close. He embraces me and kisses my neck, moves along my jawline, and finds my mouth as well. Our three tongues entangle and suck each other until they relish the taste.

I feel the blond guy fumbling with my belt until he unbuckles it, unfastening it, and pulling down my pants, using his foot as leverage so I can get rid of them. The other guy takes off my shirt until I'm trapped between the two of them, only dressed in my underwear, which showcases the size of my impressive dick, askew to the left, lifting the edge of the underwear, and the tip slightly staining the fabric with precum near my hip.

The caresses on my body multiply as the guy in the multicolored shirt gets down on his knees and presses his face against that single piece of fabric, tracing its path with his tongue.

I glance down while the other guy momentarily backs away to remove his shirt and pants, then presses against me again, this time at my side, to caress my chest while never stopping kissing me. The blond guy lifts the leg hole of my underwear slightly, letting a part of my dick slip through. I see him smiling, and it excites me. So much so that I push the other guy, the dark-haired one, on the shoulder, urging him to go down to the same spot and assist in his task.

My underwear lasts only a moment, and when my dick is exposed in all its length, both of them dive in to suck it, to kiss it. It enters and disappears into one mouth. Then into another. And later, I feel my balls in someone's mouth while the full length of my phallus is sucked at the same time.

I close my eyes and let him do with me what he wants. Suddenly, there's a flash in my mind. The image of Ben in the mountain hotel comes to me. His naked body, exposed, delicious. It excites me even more, to the point that I slightly push them away.

"Let's go to bed," I pronounce with a hoarse voice. "I want to fuck both of you."

The blond giggles with desire as he stands up and begins to undress hastily. The other stands up, kisses me, and escorts me to bed.

Soon we are all three together, squirming with pleasure. I am the center of all their acts. I don't know who is blowing me, who is kissing me, who is nibbling on my nipples.

I decide to act. I spit on my hand and look for the blonde. He's the one who doesn't stop sucking and I have his dick very close to his face. She is small and pretty, with very blonde hair. I ignore her and open his legs, until I search his anus with my fingers. He groans realizing what I'm going to do. Touching that delicious, soft skin that yields to my touch excites me even more.

I grope with a finger, which gives easily. I feel the inside of it, the resistance of the second sphincter, which also gives way, and my finger is inside without difficulty. I hear him groan as he sits up. I look at him for a moment. He is kissing his boyfriend, who in turn is masturbating both of us.

I insert a second finger. And I try with a third party.

"Fuck," he groans, "fuck me."

His wish is my command. I take him by the hips to climb him on top. He reacts to all my demands. Once located I take the dick and point where my fingers have been before. He is the one who does the rest. Who measures how far he is willing to dilate, who puts it all.

I start fucking him with desire. We looked at each other's eyes. Sex suits you. Flushed cheeks and bright eyes. The other one sucks my balls. Then he blows his boyfriend, to finish, straddling my face so he can eat my ass.

I devour it as if it were a ripe fruit, wetting it, biting, making my tongue go inside.

I hear them moan while I speed up the movements with my dick and with my mouth.

When I think they're ready, I separate.

They look at me somewhat strangely, but I smile at them and give them instructions on what I want to do.

Sounds like a great idea to them.

The blonde kneels on the floor, with his torso on the bed.

His boyfriend gets behind him and put it easily. Although he has a nice dick, it's not comparable to mine, and I have already done the hard work for him. He fucks him hard, moaning with each thrust.

Finally, I get behind and fuck the brunette.

He is tighter, and it's hard for me. But I am patient enough to enter little by little, kissing his back, biting his side, sucking on the nape of his neck.

When I have it strung, the magic happens. The three of us move in unison, as if we were one. We get up, to get on our knees and be able to kiss while we fuck.

The dark-haired man grabs his boyfriend's dick and starts masturbating it. I reach out his hand and caress his balls. They are small, soft, delicious.

We don't last long. We let each other know when he's coming. We hold on until we're ready, and the dark-haired one is the first to cum. With each blow, his sphincter contracts, which gives me even more pleasure. He moans until he is very still, but at that moment the blond ejaculates. I am surprised by the abundance of the stream of thick white milk that falls on the sheets, in several contractions, rhythmic and agonic.

I hold the blond boy's hips, pulling him towards me, so that the brunette's ass doesn't escape me.

I speed up the pace, and soon the orgasm comes. I squeeze my eyes shut as a hoarse moan escapes my lips and the image of Ben flashes through my mind again.

I imagine that I am inside him, that what my dick is going through is that closed opening between his buttocks.

It's a good orgasm. So much so that when I move away, a stream of cum still comes out of my dick and splashes down that boy's lower back.

We lay on the bed, trying to match the rhythm of our breathing.

"It's been a blast," says the dark-haired man.

"It's been a long time since we had a partner like you," the blonde confirms.

They both look at me.

"I have to go," and I stand up.

"Do not go. We can keep doing it until the sun comes up."

"But I have to go."

And I get dressed in a hurry, while those two boys kiss each other to fall asleep.

# CHAPTER 21

My life has been turned upside down.

Just a few weeks ago, I was a guy with an acceptable existence, whose only concern was surpassing a new record swimming, or running, or pedaling.

With Ben's arrival, I find myself in an unknown place in the world, or perhaps ignored, but one that I know I am a part of.

I arrived home well into the early morning. The journey back was a mix of the drowsiness from a sexual skirmish and the Nina Simone music vomiting from the radio. That allowed me to drive miles without having to think, just letting myself feel.

As soon as I arrived, I took a long shower. I don't know, maybe an hour under the hot water, as if I needed to shed my skin.

Without sleeping, I put on my sports clothes and head to the gym. Old Bill opens at six, and I don't have to be at work until eight.

The locker room is deserted, and so is the pool. It's still dark, and I'm grateful that the music hasn't been turned on, which usually pounds us with heavy metal or 80s movie soundtracks.

I dive into the water and start swimming laps. Physical exercise has always been like a lifesaver for me. It kept me away from smoking, saved me from weed, coke, and possibly heroin, which many of my schoolmates fell into. It also saved me from places like the one I went to yesterday. Not save, that would be unfair..., it changed my focus so I wouldn't see them, and the questions could be transferred to this moment I find myself in.

I don't know how long I've been in the pool. My head is under the water, and when I reach the wall to turn and swim another lap, I come across some submerged feet.

I stop and lift my head.

Ben is there, sitting on the edge, wearing his swimsuit, with a sad smile in his eyes.

"We had the same idea," he says to me.

In response, I get out of the water and sit next to him. We remain silent for a moment, our gaze lost on the rippling surface of the pool.

"I called you," he reveals, "yesterday when you left. I tried to talk to you several times."

"I turned off my phone in case that happened."

"I have no idea what terms we're on, you and I. I also don't know what happened yesterday."

He's referring to when I went to his place and left him standing after having sex in a filthy alley.

"I needed to know if what I feel for you is just a desire for sex or if there's something more," I confess.

He looks at me. His eyes are the brightest I've ever seen. When he looks at me, like now, I feel like he sees beyond me, to a Jacob that I can't even glimpse.

"And do you already know?" he asks, a tone of fear in each word.

I nod.

"I'm pretty clear about it."

He smiles. I feel the urge to kiss him. He's a magnificent specimen of a man, and yet seems like a boy next to me, trying to avoid being punished by the teacher.

"Are you going to tell me?" he dares to ask.

"No."

He smiles and plays with his feet in the water. The warm droplets splash on me, and I like it. We remain silent for a few more moments. Once again, he speaks, while I struggle to understand what I'm feeling.

"Yesterday I talked to Sharon, and I told her everything."

I turn to him.

"About yours... about us?"

"Everything."

I analyze his face. The trace of pain is recognizable in the bitter grimace of his mouth. Until this moment, I haven't realized.

"Are you okay?" I ask him, not daring to touch him, to put a hand on his shoulders, which is what I feel like doing.

He shrinks.

"No and yes," he stops. He needs to sort out his thoughts. "Bad for the harm I've caused, and good because an oppression that I was not even aware that I was with me has disappeared."

It's hard to know how he feels. Although I went through a similar situation two days ago. But it all depends on the other person and how they cope with feeling cheated.

"She'll forgive you in the end," I assure him, so he doesn't suffer, "or at least understand you."

He nods. It's something he already knows. That reassures me, because it indicates that the conversation has been civilized.

"She's coming back to the city today. We had breakfast together," he looks at me again, "I'll tough it out until the end of the month, and then move in with my parents."

Now it's me who stays observing him. I know my eyebrows are furrowed, and I must look ridiculous with the swimming cap and the goggles pressed against my forehead. When I speak, I try not to sound melodramatic, as if it weren't terrible news.

"So, you're leaving."

"Yes," he plays with his feet in the water again, "and I'm sorry if all of this has been uncomfortable for you."

Now or never.

I've turned my life upside down for a reason, and Ben has a lot to do with it. Yes, now or never.

"Yesterday, I went to a boys' bar. Burlesque. Do you know it?"

"No."

He furrows his brow, like me, and his back becomes somewhat rigid. It's not news he likes hearing.

"I met two guys, and I went to their place with them."

He wrinkles his mouth and raises a hand in a gesture of rejection.

"I'd prefer if you didn't tell me."

I ignore him.

"We had sex, and I had a good time..."

For a moment, I think he's going to stand up and leave. I'm sure he's considering it. His cheeks have flushed, and he's crossed his arms over his chest. He looks at me in a different way, swallowing saliva.

"I know that for you all of this is an adventure," he tries to remain calm, "but I told you that what I feel for you isn't just the desire to fuck you, although there's a lot of that," he smiles sadly, "It's something more. And it doesn't do me much good to know that you're fooling around with others."

I ignore him again. It's dawn, and the sky is ablaze with red over the transparent cover of the pool.

"Tonight, at certain moments," I say to the air, as if I'm addressing that prodigy of dawn, "and when I climaxed, there was only one image in my mind. Then I realized that I was enjoying it because I imagined that the person I had between my legs," I look into his eyes, "was you."

He exhales, because he was holding his breath, and slowly smiles. He lowers his head in a charming way that makes me want to hug him, kiss him. When he looks at me, there's no trace of pain.

"I hate those two guys," he declares with humor and sincerity.

"I had to do it," and I don't say it to make excuses, "I needed to figure out where my heart is."

Silence again.

Both of us are aware that one inappropriate word at this moment will shape the path we take for the rest of our lives.

"What are you going to do?" he asks me.

"Do you like this town?" I reply with another question.

"Yes, very much. Have I told you that I used to come here with my parents for summer vacations when I was a child?"

I think so. Or maybe Mark mentioned it in some of the conversations before we met. When he was trying to convince me of what a great signing the new guy was.

I place a hand on his knee and search for his eyes again.

"Stay," I say very slowly, so there are no ambiguities. "Live with me. Let's see what happens between you and me."

He raises his eyebrows.

"Are you asking me out? Just like that."

I know I've blushed. I didn't even ask Sue for something like this. We just started seeing each other more often. But with Ben, I want him to know that there's a commitment on my part.

"We might end up arguing," I warn him, "or you might leave me in a week because I'm unbearable. But there's also a possibility that this might work."

I can almost hear the commotion in his head as he tries to understand. He came here for a farewell, and it's possible that he'll leave the pool with a... boyfriend?

"Would you be ready for something like that?" he asks me.

I'm from a small town. I live in a small town. But if I've told Sue and Mark, and nothing has caught fire, I can handle anything.

"I've fucked two guys in their twenties to figure it out," I wink at him, "so the answer is yes."

He sighs and presses his lips together.

I feel my heart pounding.

"Only under one condition," he finally says.

"Tell me," I impatiently urge him.

He makes me wait while in my head, I pray for him to say "yes, yes, yes."

"That you only fuck me."

And I throw myself at his mouth, his lips, with such desire that my soul aches for Ben.

Thank you. If you liked it, you could help me spread it by leaving a review.

This QR code will take you to the Amazon review page.

Printed in Great Britain
by Amazon

40429873R00071